AS THE CLOCK TICKED ON...

Miss Unwin's heart leapt up at Vilkins's announcement of the annual ball at General Pastell's. As she had sat eating her gluey-cold supper, thinking over all she had learnt in her reading of the newspaper accounts of Jack Steadman's trial and fearing that ex-Superintendent Heavitree would never concur with her belief in his innocence, she had felt minute by minute an increasing despair. Yes, she did not waver by a hairsbreadth in her conviction that Jack Steadman had not killed Alfie Goode. But, as strongly, she thought of the appealingly short time there was before Jack Steadman was to be hanged. Four days only. Four short days.

But now, not only had Mr. Heavitree unexpectedly backed her, but there had been put before her a way in which she could at least get a glimpse of all the possible alternative suspects within the course of a single evening. Next evening ... at General Pastell's.

INTO THE VALLEY OF DEATH

OF DEATH

H.R.F. KEATING WRITING AS EVELYN HERVEY

BERKLEY BOOKS, NEW YORK

All of the characters in this book
are fictitious, and any resemblance
to actual persons, living or dead, is purely coincidental.

This Berkley book contains the complete
text of the original hardcover edition.

INTO THE VALLEY OF DEATH

A Berkley Book/published by arrangement with Doubleday,
a division of Bantam Doubleday Dell Publishing Group, Inc.

PRINTING HISTORY
Doubleday edition/July 1986
Berkley edition/September 1989

ISBN: 0-425-11743-X

A BERKLEY BOOK ® TM 757,375
Berkley Books are published by The Berkley Publishing Group,
200 Madison Avenue, New York, New York 10016.
The name "BERKLEY" and the "B" logo
are trademarks belonging to Berkley Publishing Corporation.
PRINTED IN THE UNITED STATES OF AMERICA

10 9 8 7 6 5 4 3 2 1

Author's Note:
Connoisseurs of crime fiction may feel as they read this book that they have been here before. They have, at least in part: in Philip MacDonald's excellent story of 1930, "The Noose." I am happy to acknowledge having pillaged something of its admirable plot.

INTO THE VALLEY OF DEATH

1

Miss Unwin took a hansom. If she could get to the Paddington Station in a quarter of an hour, she calculated, she might yet catch the only train that would get her before late evening on this Sunday to the Valley of Death.

She reached up with her cotton umbrella and tapped sharply on the hood of the gently swaying vehicle. From his high perch at her back, the driver opened the little communicating panel in the roof above her.

"Cannot you go at any better speed?" she asked. "There's half a crown on top of your fare if you get me there in time."

"I'm a-doing my best, ain't I, miss?" the cabbie grunted, slamming the panel down again.

But Miss Unwin noted that at once he flicked his long whip onto the horse in front of her and sent their lightweight vehicle skimming through the almost deserted London streets, lapped by the soft ringing of church-bells, a great deal more quickly than before.

With a fine clatter of hooves on the cobbles at last, they drew up at the station with three or four minutes more in hand than Miss Unwin had counted on. She thrust the fare money, and that extra half-crown, up through the roof to the cabbie, pushed open the low doors in front of her, and stepped briskly down.

Quickly she looked this way and that and in a moment spotted a porter dawdling his way towards a cluster of passengers surrounded by heaps of luggage, corded trunks, valises, hatboxes, portmanteaus, bandboxes, Gladstone bags, baskets, and parcels. She raised her umbrella high, careless of dignity, and called loudly, "Porter! Porter!"

The man, scenting a good tip, nipped round the party of travellers and came up to Miss Unwin at a trot.

He touched his uniform cap. "At your service, miss."

"Take my bag," Miss Unwin said, indicating the solitary carpet-bag on the rack of the hansom, all that she had had time to pack. "First to the ticket office, and then to the train for Chipping Compton."

"Yes, miss," the man answered. "Platform three it is."

At as fast a walk as was compatible with ladylike behaviour, Miss Unwin followed the porter, her bag up on his shoulder, to the ticket office, found to her relief that no other travellers were there before her, purchased a second-class ticket, and turned to go to the train.

"You'll 'ave to hurry, miss," the porter said. "Her'll be off in a minute."

"No," she said, consulting the watch pinned to the bosom of her neat alpaca dress. "We have quite three minutes. That will be time enough."

However urgent the need, she was not going to be bullied into more speed, and a larger tip, than was necessary.

The porter glowered. But he made no further attempt to chivvy her.

They passed the barrier at the platform, went rapidly but not over-rapidly along the length of the train towards the great steam-shrouded locomotive, and found a second-class compartment occupied by only a single, somewhat elderly, respectable-looking man. The porter entered, heaved Miss Unwin's bag onto the rack, and stood waiting with his hand held out. Miss Unwin put into it a nicely calculated sum. The porter, with surprised gratitude, touched his cap, got down, and closed the carriage door without the heavy slam he had expected to bestow on it as a mark of disapproval.

The guard's whistle shrilled out. The long train gave a shudder back and forwards and slowly got into motion.

Miss Unwin settled in her seat and took from her reticule the telegraphic message she had received early that morning.

Come to Valley of Death quick as you can. Help wanted. Signed Vilkins.

She read the words over two or three times, but they meant no more to her than they had when the telegraph boy, his whistling loud in the Sunday quiet, had brought the message to the house where she was governess.

But she was still clear in her mind that the message had to be answered as quickly as possible by her own presence down in Oxfordshire. Because the call for help had come from her oldest friend in all the world, the person who as an infant only a few days old had been named by the beadle in charge of the workhouse where they had both been found-lings as "Vilkins" to follow in alphabetical order the "Unwin" he had bestowed on herself. Vilkins, who was now a house-maid in the country after twice working where Miss Unwin herself had been governess, had the right to call on her for immediate assistance if ever anyone had.

Yet it was a piece of luck that she had been in a position to go to her at once. Her present charge, the Honourable Ronald Adair, aged five, had been taken by his parents for the summer to cousins in Scotland, where she was not required. It was to provide some diversion during the long hot weeks in the airless Mayfair house with the servants on board wages as her only company that she had written just a few days before to Vilkins suggesting a visit when her friend had an afternoon off.

But instead of the expected reply, written for Vilkins by one of her better-educated fellow servants, there had come this urgent and inexplicable message.

The Valley of Death. What was that? Where was it?

She had looked in haste at the *Atlas of the English Counties* in her employer's library when the telegram had come and there had certainly been no such name there. Monkton

Hall, where Vilkins worked, had appeared to be in a small valley. But in the atlas that had been clearly marked as the Vale of Monkton.

The only Valley of Death that Miss Unwin knew of was that in Mr. Tennyson's famous verses.

> Half a league, half a league,
> Half a league onward,
> All in the valley of Death
> Rode the six hundred.
> "Forward, the Light Brigade!"

Curious that not so long ago she had read the very poem to little Ronald. It was there in the front of the book of tales of the famous Light Brigade charge, of the smoke-shrouded Battle of the Alma and of the storming of Sebastopol which the boy had been given for his birthday, *Heroes of the Crimea* by the Rev. C. P. Wilkinson. But the Valley of Death there was in distant Russia, and the charge of the Light Brigade had taken place more than twenty years before. Nothing of that, surely, could be what had caused Vilkins to dictate that message of hers at the nearest telegraph office.

Help wanted.

Well, if Vilkins had asked for help, help she should have, to the utmost of Miss Unwin's abilities. But what was it that she could want help over?

Still, no amount of thinking would produce an answer now. For that she would have to wait till she reached Chipping Compton. No doubt, there she would be able to hire a fly and get herself taken to Monkton Hall. With the generous remuneration she now had, at least she was not hampered for lack of money.

From her reticule she took the only book she had had time to cram into it when she had decided, at barely a minute's notice, to try to catch the train. *The Child's Guide to Useful Knowledge*. She settled down to read. She must acquaint herself with what in its pages she should pass on to the young

Honourable Ronald when after the languid dog days he returned to her care.

The hours of the journey slowly passed.

The portly man in the opposite corner of the carriage emerged once from behind yesterday's rather vulgar *Mercury* newspaper to ask whether she would mind if he lowered the window "in all this 'eat." Miss Unwin, deciding he was probably a commercial gentleman of some sort, agreed that it was hot and that an open window would be pleasant. She resumed her study of the useful knowledge that might benefit the Honourable Ronald.

But from time to time she still could not prevent herself fruitlessly asking why Vilkins had sent her the message. And the words of Mr. Tennyson's poem beat out then with maddening repetition in her mind.

> "Forward, the Light Brigade!"
> Was there a man dismayed?
> Not though the soldier knew
> Some one had blundered:
> Theirs not to make reply,
> Theirs not to reason why,
> Theirs but to do and die.
> Into the valley of Death
> Rode the six hundred.

The same words were still battering in her head when at length the train drew into a station and she heard the voice of a country porter calling out, "Chipping Compton, Chipping Compton! Alight here for Chipping Compton!"

The stout commercial gentleman was gallant enough to hand her down her carpet-bag, and in a few moments she was standing on the wooden platform wondering where she might find a fly to take her to Monkton Hall.

But when she asked the solitary porter for directions, she got a surprising answer.

"Ah, 'tis you'll be the lady her's 'specting."

"Her? Who is this? I do not think I am expected."

The porter shook his head cheerfully. "Oh, you be that all right," he said. "She be along askin' o' me when train's comin' three times already this mornin'."

"But she? Who is this?"

"Why, lass that's helping out over at Rising Sun, now landlord's been took away to be hanged."

Miss Unwin found that the answer confused her even more than she had been before. She decided there was nothing else to do but wait and see who "the lass" was. Certainly it could not be Vilkins. She was in service at Monkton Hall, not a girl helping at some public house. And what was all that about the landlord? And being taken away to be hanged? Was this why there was a Valley of Death, whatever that might be?

But as she emerged from the station into the street outside, basking in the sleepy heat of summer midday, one of her questions at least was answered. There, standing in the middle of the dusty earthen road, without a bonnet, a large sacking apron hanging at her waist, red-faced and with her big dab of a nose yet redder, was none other than Vilkins.

She hurried across.

"Vilkins," she said. "You here? How is that? And your message, what on earth did it mean?"

"Oh, Unwin, such trouble, such trouble as you ain't never 'eard the like of. An' only you can save 'im, Unwin. No one but you."

"Save whom, Vilkins dear? I don't understand a thing."

"No more you shouldn't, and no more do I. But come along to the Sun, that's the first thing."

"The Sun? The Rising Sun? A public house? And the porter at the station seemed to say you were working there? Vilkins, is that true? A public house?"

"Oh, I'll tell you all about it, Unwin. I'll tell you in a jiffy. Only I can't do it 'ere, not out in the road, can I?"

"Well, no, dear, I see that. But do I have to go to a public house? Don't forget that, whatever I once was, I am a lady now."

"Oh, Unwin, as if I could forget. That's what makes me proud, that does, that you've risen up to be a proper lady what was my best friend in them days long ago when we 'adn't got nothing but being friends to bless ourselves with. An' is that your bag?"

"Well, yes, but isn't there someone to carry it?"

"Don't talk daft, Unwin. Not you as 'as known me from the very beginning. You think I can't carry a bit of a luggage the like o' that?"

And, her brawny arm bared to the elbow, Vilkins snatched up the carpet-bag and turned to march off with it as if it was no more than a basket of eggs.

Miss Unwin followed her, even more full of doubts than when she had got out of the train.

The Rising Sun proved to be not much more than a hundred yards distant from the station on the road leading out of the town. It appeared to Miss Unwin to be a well-kept place, barring the fact that its painted sign looked more like a picture of a mustard plaster than that of King Sol emerging over the horizon, and her doubts about allowing Vilkins to take her to such a place began to dissolve.

Until she remembered what the porter at the station had said to her in that Oxfordshire accent she had found hard to understand. *Now landlord's been took away to be hanged.* If this was really a public house whose landlord deserved to be hanged, she was not at all sure that she did wish to enter it after all.

But Vilkins was not giving her any opportunity to stay outside. Still swinging her bag by its handle as if it had nothing at all in it, she marched in at the open door and tramped along a passageway giving access to the taproom on one side and the private bar on the other. At the far end there was a broad flight of stairs, and at its foot she turned round.

"The missus's sitting-room's upstairs," she said, "an' she's kept it empty for us special."

Miss Unwin, feeling happier, followed her friend up the stairs and into a room above the private bar. It was a good deal more comfortable than she had expected, with a bowl of country flowers on the round table in its middle, a sofa under the leaded window, and a pair of easy chairs on either side of the fireplace, where in the grate stood a neat folded paper ornament until summer should be over.

"You sit down there," Vilkins said, "an' rest yourself, an' I'll fetch a pot o' tea."

"No, Vilkins dear. First, for heaven's sake, tell me what all this is about."

"I will not. Tea you'll be needing after being in one o' them nasty trains all the morning, an' tea you'll get."

And, since with those words Vilkins had marched out, Miss Unwin did have to sit on the sofa where she had been put and be as patient as she could manage.

Well, she thought, I have come here as Vilkins asked. But is this the Valley of Death? It hardly seems like it. To begin with, the town is not in a valley as far as I can see, and there certainly does not seem to be any odour of death about this nice, neat-looking little room.

And, true enough, a cup of tea would be more than welcome.

She turned and tried looking out into the road beneath to see if it held any clue to the mystery Vilkins had put before her. But the road was as quiet and deserted under the tranquil sunshine as any other in all England. The only sign of life she saw—and that was not until several minutes had passed— was a yellowish dog with a black tail that came out from the shadows of the house and walked slowly across the dusty road to lie down again on the far side.

But then at last she heard Vilkins's familiar clumping tread, accompanied by the loud clink of cups on a tea tray. A moment later, pushing the door wide with her hip, her friend of old came back in again.

"And now," Miss Unwin said with all the determination she could muster, "you must and shall tell me all."

2

Vilkins set down the tea tray with a loud clatter on the round table in the middle of the room. Miss Unwin saw that on it, besides a large brown teapot and cups, saucers, and plates, there was a big, partly cut fruit-cake, its interior gleaming with raisins, currants, and walnuts. She felt a sharp pang of hunger, but thrust it aside.

"He's going to be 'anged, that's the thing," Vilkins said without preliminary. "An' it ain't right. It ain't right at all."

She snatched one of the teacups and banged it down on its saucer, as if this inanimate object was the cause of whatever it was that had stirred her to anger.

Miss Unwin jumped up from the sofa and almost seized her friend by the shoulders to shake her. "Vilkins, who? Who is to be hanged? Is it the landlord here? Was that what the porter was telling me?"

"Why, in course it's him," Vilkins answered. "Don't you never see the papers up in London now? Don't you know nothink?"

Miss Unwin, in fact, seldom did see a newspaper. Ever since once, accused of murder herself, she had been pilloried in the letters columns of *The Times*, she had had a sort of horror of all newspapers.

"No. No, my dear. I'm afraid I know nothing of what you are saying. Tell me about it all from the beginning, if you please."

"Oh, Lord," Vilkins said. "There's so much to tell, if as you 'onestly don't know a blessed word about it. I'd better pour this tea first, or it'll be stone cold afore I've 'alf done. An' you'd better 'ave a nice piece o' this cake what Mrs. Steadman baked with 'er own 'ands an' sent up special."

"Well, yes, dear. I am hungry, I confess. But Mrs. Steadman, who is she? Is she the landlady of this place? Is it her husband that you say is to be hanged?"

Vilkins, splashily pouring tea into their cups, looked up. "Now who's asking to 'ave it all back to front?" she said. "No, you wait until I gets me breath, an' then I'll tell you proper."

So Miss Unwin sat back again on the sofa and took her cup of tea and the generous slice of cake Vilkins had cut for her.

"All right," Vilkins said, plonking herself down on an upright horsehair chair at the table. "I'll tell it you right from the beginning."

She took a noisy sip from her cup.

"It all started," she said, "on a day in May last. Or rather it was a night. An' Jack Steadman—'im as is landlord 'ere, or was, if 'e ain't still—well, there 'e was out after a rabbit in the woods a mile or so from 'ere, what the General allows 'im to shoot in though them is what they calls 'is preserves."

"Vilkins, stop. I'm utterly confused already. Was it day, or was it night? And the General, who is he? And why does he allow Mr. Steadman to shoot in his preserves?"

"Well, that last I can answer," Vilkins replied. "That's along o' Mr. Steadman being Corporal Steadman as was."

"Vilkins dear, I am as much at a loss as ever. More so."

"Oh, Unwin, don't you start being stupid. It's as clear as day. General Pastell, 'im as what I works for up at Monkton Hall, naturally when 'e 'ears as what Jack Steadman's left the Army at last, 'e finds 'im this nice pub to keep, an' 'is woods being near 'e lets 'im shoot a rabbit or two for the pot whenever it so 'appens as the fit takes 'im."

"All right. Now I begin to understand. But, you say, Mr. Steadman is to be hanged? Did he commit a murder in those woods that night?"

"You got it, Unwin. I knew as you would, you being clever as any monkey, only more so. But yet you ain't."

"I haven't?"

"No. 'Cos, you see, the 'ole of it is that Jack Steadman couldn't no more of killed Alfie Goode nor what I could, an' I 'adn't never set eyes on either of 'em when it all 'appened."

"Vilkins, I'm getting confused once more."

"Well, it's easy to tell. When they come an' arrested Mr. Steadman, in course the General got to know at onct. An' being the man 'e is, what is the best o' gentlemen alive, 'e straightaway thinks o' poor Mrs. Steadman 'ere, an' 'ow will she manage without 'er 'usband. So what 'e done is 'e what 'e calls temporary detaches me."

Miss Unwin grappled with all that for a moment. "The General is good enough to send you, one of his housemaids, down here to assist Mrs. Steadman, the landlady of the Rising Sun?"

"That's what I said, didn't I?"

"Well, so far I have it clear. But, Vilkins, why did you send me a telegram? And what is the Valley of Death where I am supposed to have come?"

"Well," Vilkins answered, "it ain't the Valley o' Death really in a manner o' speaking. In course it ain't. 'Ow could it be?"

"Then why did you call it so?"

" 'Cos that's what it is. That's what it is to a T. I mean, what's them woods called? The Hanger, ain't they? Hanger Woods. An' up at the top beyond 'em what did they 'ave not so long ago but a gallows? So what else will the countryfolk round 'ere call that valley where Alfie Goode met 'is end but the Valley o' Death? It's Monkton Vale proper, so Mrs. Perker, the 'ousekeeper at the Hall, once told me. But to one an' all round 'ere it's the Valley o' Death, an' so it ought to be."

"Yes. Yes, I understand that now. But, Vilkins, why me? Why did you send for me?"

"That's easy, Unwin. That's as simple as ABC, not but what that ain't so simple to me. It's you what's got to get 'im off. An' 'e's to be 'anged on Friday morning, you know. 'Anged in less nor a week."

Miss Unwin sat back and took a deep breath. "Vilkins," she said hesitantly, "I think I begin to see what it is that has been happening down here. And I think, too, I begin to guess why you asked me to come. You think that, because twice in my life I have been caught up in cases of murder and that on both occasions it so happened I was able to point to the actual perpetrators, that—that I am somehow possessed of extraordinary powers. But, my dear, I am not. I am not indeed. And —and there's more. If your Mr. Steadman is really to be hanged in a week, then he must have been brought to trial and found guilty. Well, my dear, I suppose that there have been innocent men hanged before now, but I do not think it happens so often. So if Mr. Steadman has been tried and found to be guilty, then it is almost certain that guilty he is."

"But 'e ain't," said Vilkins.

Miss Unwin sighed. "Did you say you knew him?" she asked. "I can well understand that it's hard to believe a person one knows, and who perhaps has treated one with some kindness, can be guilty of a heinous crime. But such sometimes must be the case. Try to see it, dear, try to put it all from your mind."

"But I said," Vilkins replied, "I ain't never set eyes on Jack Steadman. Yet I knows 'e ain't guilty. I knows it as well as I knows it's you, Unwin, what's sitting there in front o' me."

"But why, Vilkins, why? How can you know such a thing so firmly?"

" 'Cos o' Mrs. Steadman, in course. 'Cos of 'er an' no one else."

"Mrs. Steadman?"

"Why, yes. Yes. Ain't she the soul o' goodness? Ain't she as honest a woman as ever I met? Ain't she one as would say, an' say straight out, if she thought that a 'usband of hers 'ad done somethink bad? But she don't, Unwin. She don't. It's just the opposite what she says. She says as 'er Jack couldn't never of done it, an' I believes 'er, an' so will you onct you sees 'er. That you will."

Miss Unwin sat and thought. And at last she spoke. "Well, my dear, I think there is only one thing for it. I will see Mrs. Steadman. I will ask her to tell me why it is she thinks her husband, who is to be hanged in less than a week, cannot be guilty of what he has been charged with. And then I will make up my own mind."

She rose from the sofa and went across and laid her hand on her friend's bony shoulder. "But, my dear," she said, "you must not think that it is really likely that I shall find myself agreeing with you and with her. And even if I do, what will there be that I can find out that the police and the lawyers for the defence and the assizes judge in his wisdom have not looked into before me? And in less than a week. From Sunday only till Friday, till Thursday if I am to be in time."

But Vilkins turned her large red globe of a face towards her and gave her a look of pure, warm belief. "You'll do it, Unwin," she said. "You'll do it, 'cos you're you."

Then she leapt up, half upsetting her chair, and blundered out. And less than two minutes later Mrs. Steadman opened the door.

She was a very small person, barely five feet in height. But she stood upright as a ramrod. And her little round face was, Miss Unwin thought, red and bright as an apple.

Then she corrected herself. Not red as an apple. But red and brightly sharp as a crab-apple.

"Mrs. Steadman," she burst out before her hostess had had time to speak a word. "Mrs. Steadman, I have just learnt of the terrible situation in which you find yourself. Let me say at once, whatever the rights or the wrongs of it, that I feel for you. I wish— Oh, I wish that it could all be otherwise."

"But it ain't," said Mrs. Steadman. "It just ain't, and that's got to be faced up to, the same as I faced up to all the dangers and hardships when I was with my Jack all round the whole wide world, when we was wet and weary in Ireland, when we was hot and thirsty in India, when my poor lad was missing nigh on a month after the Battle of the Alma. I faced up to it then, and I'll face up to it now."

Miss Unwin could at once see her facing those hardships and those dangers, and facing them with unabated cheerfulness. Resolution and brightness radiated from that small upright form, that battered but bright-cheeked face.

"I suppose my poor, good friend has told you something of myself," Miss Unwin said. "And I am sadly afraid she will have told you more than the simple truth. Yes, she knows that I have, twice even, unravelled mysteries that were deep indeed. But, believe me, Mrs. Steadman, I am no miracle worker. I chanced before to see in the end the logic of what was there to be seen, but I could do no more. And—and— But perhaps you should tell me the circumstances of your trouble. Dear Vilkins has hardly done that."

"Let's sit down, me dear," Mrs. Steadman answered. "You take the chair there under the china dog on the mantel and I —I'll sit where my dear Jack sits of a Sunday when we're at leisure, and I'll tell you all that's to be told."

Miss Unwin went and put herself in the chair over which there presided a bright brown-and-white china dog with a collar of gold paint. Her hostess sat, a small fierce figure, in the big chair opposite.

"There's not so much to tell," Mrs. Steadman said, "when it comes down to it. And black against my Jack the telling makes it, as I well know. But kill that Alfie Goode he did not, for all that the man deserved to be killed if ever man did."

"I know hardly anything of the circumstances," Miss Unwin said.

"You know that it happened in the place they call Hanger Wood, down in the valley not much more'n a mile from the house?"

"Yes."

"Well, there early one morning, at the beginning of this

May as ever was, a keeper in General Pastell's employ found as he walked the woods two bodies lying in a glade."

"Two bodies?"

"Yes, two. One with the back of his head shot away, dead as mutton. And the other lying there as if dead, but, when the keeper came to touch him, well alive, though he had struck his head on the stump of an oak and was senseless to the world. My husband, my Jack. My Jack with a shotgun, his own blessed shotgun, by his side and, as the keeper soon found, discharged."

"And what is supposed to have happened?"

"They said at the inquest and again at the trial—and you shall if you want 'em see the newspapers that printed near every word that was uttered at either—they said that my Jack had shot that man, who he had quarrelled with, as I well know, had shot him, and then in the dark, seeking to leave the place, had stumbled and by chance had struck his head on that oak stump and had lain there for all the world to see him in his villainy."

"And Mr. Steadman," Miss Unwin asked, "when he had come to his senses, what had he to say?"

"Why, that he had done no such thing as they said of him, of course."

"But how did he account for the circumstances? They look black on the face of it, as you must know."

"He told them that he had been walking in the woods, as he often did of a night when we had closed the doors of the house, to get some air, and that something—he knows not what—struck him on the head and that afterwards he knew no more."

"And he could offer no other explanation?"

"He said he had told the truth and that should be enough for anybody. And so it should, Miss Unwin, because if Jack said it, it is God's own truth and that alone."

Little Mrs. Steadman sat so upright in the big armchair that belonged to her husband and looked so steadily and truly at her from a pair of the brightest and bluest of eyes that Miss Unwin knew then that she was indeed being told the pure and simple truth.

"Mrs. Steadman," she said at once, "I cannot, of course, see how those black circumstances can be other than they seem. But, yes, I will take your word for it that they are. If you tell me your husband is guiltless, I will believe it."

"And guiltless he is," Mrs. Steadman replied. "Alfie Goode was shot, as I told you, in the back of the head. If my Jack ever had to shoot a man—and in battle he has done that, God forgive him—then he would do it face-to-face. Face-to-face as he met the Indian hordes and the Russian Cossacks in their might."

"He fought in India and in Russia," Miss Unwin said, "and yet you believe that he did not kill that man in Hanger Wood?"

"I do. I believe it as certain as I am sitting here in his chair. I shall believe it to my dying day. But—but there's one more thing you must know. One more thing that looks more damning than the rest."

"Yes? What is it?"

"Why, in my Jack's pocket when they came to search him they found a note."

"A note?"

"Yes, from that villain Alfie Goode. And, Miss Unwin, it was a note in Alfie Goode's own hand, as was proved and proved twice over. A note saying to meet him in Hanger Wood that night."

"And what does your husband say to that?"

"That he never set eyes on it in his life. That and no more."

"I see. And, let me ask once again, you still believe him to be innocent?"

"As a new-born babe. Still I believe it."

Miss Unwin, sitting there opposite her, thought then that somehow, battered old woman of more than fifty summers though she was, she too was a new-born babe for pure innocence. She could not lie and deceive. She would not have lied and deceived to save her husband, precious to her though he was, if she knew him to be other than guiltless of the charge against him.

And he was to be hanged on Friday.

"Mrs. Steadman," she said, "what I can do I will do. As heaven is my witness it must be little enough, and there is little enough time to do it in. But to the best of my powers all that I can do to prove your husband innocent, that I will do."

3

For all the fierce belief in Jack Steadman's innocence that Miss Unwin had gained from little, blue-eyed, crab-apple-cheeked Mrs. Steadman, the power of logical thought she had inherited from one or the other of her unknown parents was as strong in her as ever.

"Mrs. Steadman," she said after they had sat in silence for more than a few moments, "though I have come to believe every word you have said about your husband—that he is indeed a man incapable of shooting another in the back—yet there is still something, I find, that I must do before I begin so much as to think how, in the terribly short time we have, his name can be cleared."

"You do what you think right, me dear," Mrs. Steadman answered. "You do that."

"Then as quickly as may be I must talk to some other people who know your husband. I must find for myself an unclouded view of him. Do you see that? Then, if they confirm what you have told me, and I don't doubt that they can, I will do all that I may though I do not sleep from now till next Thursday night."

"Yes, that I understand," Mrs. Steadman answered. "And I can give you names by the score as'll vouch for my Jack. Why, there's General Pastell himself up at the Hall for a beginning."

"No," said Miss Unwin.

"No? You're not afraid o' asking to see the General, are you? There's no need. He'd do anything to see justice for Jack. He got up a petition, you know."

"A petition? And it has been presented?"

Mrs. Steadman, bolt upright in her big armchair, gave a puff of a sigh that had in it more of exasperation than of sadness.

"Presented it was," she said. "To the Home Sekertairy himself. And rejected it was. Out of hand. 'Nothing in the evidence,' he said. 'Nothing in the evidence.' "

It was Miss Unwin's turn to sigh now. "Yes," she said, "you must face this, Mrs. Steadman. There hardly will be anything in the evidence that has been found so far to give us a chance of gaining a reprieve. There cannot really have been."

"I know it, I know it," Mrs. Steadman answered.

Looking at her sitting there, eyes straight to the front, facing what had to be faced as she had no doubt faced all the hardships of a soldier's wife in cantonment and campaign, Miss Unwin saw her as every bit as brave as her husband or any of the soldiers of that last war peaceful England had fought. She saw her, indeed, as one of those gallant Six Hundred charging the guns in the Valley of Death.

> Cannon to the right of them,
> Cannon to the left of them,
> Cannon in front of them
> Volleyed and thundered;
> Stormed at with shot and shell,
> Boldly they rode and well,
> Into the jaws of Death,
> Into the mouth of Hell . . .

But she hardened her heart.

"No," she said. "No, Mrs. Steadman, I must not go to anyone you recommend to me. I must go to those I find for myself."

She left then and went quietly down to the entrance passage of the house. There she looked about her, first into the private bar, then into the taproom. There she thought she saw what she wanted.

On this sleepy Sunday afternoon the room was nearly deserted, but for a maid, a big-boned, buxom fresh-faced creature, lazily sweeping sawdust onto the brick floor ready for the evening's customers.

Miss Unwin stepped in. "Good afternoon," she said.

The girl turned to see who had spoken. And when she saw Miss Unwin, a deep, dark blush spread up suddenly all over her sturdy neck, blue-white as fresh milk, and up onto her rosy cheeks.

"You may be able to give me some help," Miss Unwin said to her. "Tell me, have you lived here in Chipping Compton all your life?"

The girl looked puzzled. The deep blush began slowly to fade.

"Why, yes, miss," she answered in a twangy Oxfordshire accent. "That I have. Twenty-two year come Michaelmas."

"Good. Then I expect you will be able to tell me what it is I want to know."

Miss Unwin advanced farther into the room and pushed its heavy oak door partially closed.

"You know what a situation Mrs. Steadman is in, of course?" she asked.

"Oh, yes. Yes, miss, I do. And Mary Vilkins a-telling me, like as a secret, that you come down special to get Mr. Steadman off."

Inwardly Miss Unwin winced. She would much have preferred it if Vilkins had told no single soul the purpose of her visit, especially before she had made up her mind that there was anything that she could do. But the damage had been done.

It must have been the knowledge of the shared secret, she guessed, that had brought up that deep blush on the girl's cheeks.

"Yes," she said to her, "I am here at Mary's request to see if there is anything yet to be done. And you can perhaps help me."

The deep-red blush came up again on the rosy face.

"Oh, don't worry," Miss Unwin hastened to say. "What I am asking is simple enough."

The blush retreated.

"All I want from you," Miss Unwin went on, "is to be told of some two or three people in the town who have known Mr. Steadman well. Do not tell me, if you can avoid it, of those who especially liked him. Tell me even the names of people who have not much cause to sympathise with him, if you can."

A look of slow thought planted itself on the girl's face.

"Why," she said at last, "there's Parson, o' course. He's been parson o' the parish, they say, for forty year an' more, and he hasn't got no special cause to like Mr. Steadman, Mr. Steadman being what they calls in church a publican and sinner."

"Good. The parson. What is his name?"

"Oh, ay. That be Reverend Dr. Clarke."

"Good. Now, who else?"

"Well, if you be wanting the one as has known Jack Steadman longest of all, then there's no one better nor old Mrs. Orridge."

"Mrs. Orridge. And who is she that she should have known Mr. Steadman so long?"

The girl gave a gurgle of laughter. "Why, she be midwife what brought 'un into world, she be."

Miss Unwin smiled in her turn. "Yes, no one better. And don't bother your head too much, but is there perhaps one other?"

Again the girl stood leaning on her broom, a picture of slowly churning thought.

"Why, no," she said at last. "No, I can't think— Why, why, yes, there be."

"And who is that?"

"Mr. Sprunge, o' course. Old Mr. Sprunge what's been

beadle o' the parish nigh on as long as Dr. Clarke's been parson."

And at the mention of Mr. Sprunge's office Miss Unwin's heart sank. A beadle was to her of all mankind the one she could not do other than hate and even fear. Parish orphan herself until she had been lucky enough to be sent as kitchen-maid to a good home, a beadle was for ever a figure of dread in her eyes. She had suffered, suffered time and again, at the hands of the beadle of her parish, and she could not but think of anyone holding such an office—in charge of workhouse discipline, responsible for keeping order in church—except with real fear.

Yet if anyone here could tell her of Jack Steadman's true character, was it not likely that it would be the man who had been beadle since Jack was a boy?

She asked the girl, whose name she learnt was Betsey, where she could find first Mr. Sprunge, then Mrs. Orridge, and finally the parson.

Then without delay she set out into the sleepy Sunday streets of the little town, their quiet disturbed only by the lazy cooing of the occasional pigeon from the deep green depths of the still trees.

The beadle lived, as had the beadle who had made her own early days a misery, in a cottage next to the parish work-house, and it was the necessity of visiting Mr. Sprunge there that added yet more to her almost sick feeling of revulsion. But from Mr. Sprunge she was likely to hear what she must know if she was to help Mrs. Steadman. So without hesitation she marched along till she came to his cottage.

At its door she forced herself to tap at once with the brightly polished brass knocker, and only thought that in her time she had been the one often to have rubbed and rubbed at such a knocker and to have been punished unfairly often enough when after her work was done something had blemished its shine.

The door was opened almost at once by the beadle himself.

Miss Unwin saw that he wore just such a fine coat with gold
lacing on cuffs and collar as she had dreaded seeing in her
childhood. But at least the man inside it was not as fat and
puffed-angry of visage as the beadle she had known. He was
tall, evidently grave, with a settled, cone-shaped face that
even had something of an air of benevolence.

"Mr. Sprunge?"

"Madam?"

"Mr. Sprunge, I must ask you to forgive me for intruding
upon you on a Sunday."

Mr. Sprunge gravely nodded his large head once in acknowledgement of this politeness.

But in her anxiety about the encounter, Miss Unwin had
failed to prepare any excuse for asking about Jack Steadman.
In the heat of the moment, however, words came to her.

"I am a representative of the *Englishwoman's Domestic
Magazine,*" she said boldly.

"Indeed, madam."

"Indeed. And it has come to the notice of our editress that
there has been in your town a case of murder of considerable
interest. She has for long wished to see in the magazine's
pages an article on the position and feelings of the wife of a
man of some respectability who is under sentence of death,
and she has commissioned me now to come here to see what I
can find."

"Indeed, madam," Mr. Sprunge said, even more gravely
than before, if that were possible.

Miss Unwin plunged on, hard though she found the going.

"Yes, sir. And I am anxious first to acquaint myself with
more of the circumstances before I approach Mrs. Steadman
—is that the name?—before I approach Mrs. Steadman herself."

"Indeed, madam?"

"Yes."

Miss Unwin drew a weary breath. "Yes, sir. So I have come
to you as being, I understand, the person in the town most

able to give me an account, not of the case itself, the details of which I have learnt from the newspapers, but of the man who has been found guilty of the crime."

"That is, Mr. Steadman? John Steadman of this parish?"

"Exactly. Now, would you be able to tell me something about him? As the parish beadle, you would know more of him than perhaps anyone here."

The gross flattery seemed to work. Onto Mr. Sprunge's solemn cone of a face there came a look of profound thought.

"Yes, madam," he said at last. "Yes, I consider that I am that man."

"And?"

"And, madam?"

"And what can you tell me of John Steadman?"

"Ah. Ah, yes."

More deep consideration. Then a long-drawn breath. "What I shall tell you, madam, will, I truly believe, astonish you."

Miss Unwin drew herself up. "I am ready to be astonished," she said.

"Then, madam, I will say this. This and no more. John Steadman, convicted murderer though he be, is a truly good man. A truly good boy he was when I marched him to sing in the choir at church, and a truly good man he has proved ever since he came back to this town of ours from serving Her Majesty the Queen in a military capacity. There, madam."

Miss Unwin duly put on a display of fine astonishment. Mr. Sprunge appeared gratified. She thanked him then for his assistance and, seeing the spire of the parish church not far distant, set off in the direction of the rectory and the Reverend Dr. Clarke.

Her interviews with him and with old Mrs. Orridge, the midwife, who proved to be a terrible gossip, were longer by a good deal than her encounter with the beadle. But neither did anything to take away from the impression she had formed from pompous Mr. Sprunge.

"Yes," Dr. Clarke, pink-faced and white-haired, had declared at the end. "Steadman, though he keeps an inn, is as fine a fellow as you will come across in all Oxfordshire. I cannot understand how he can have done such a fearful thing, and only the evidence in court persuades me that he did."

While Mrs. Orridge, in her way, was as positive. "Oh, little Jack Steadman would knock down a boy in fight like a true 'un, so he would. But in fair fight always, mind you. In fair fight and no hard words after. That was Jack Steadman."

Miss Unwin hurried back to the Rising Sun after this. Much of this hot July Sunday had gone, and next Friday at eight o'clock in the morning Jack Steadman, the fair fighter, would be led out to the hangman's noose.

Yet she could find in her mind little notion how she might set about the task she had undertaken. It was all very well for Vilkins to believe she was some sort of magician who had only to look at the facts of a case to be able to put a completely different interpretation on them from everybody else, and the true interpretation at that. It was all very well for indomitable Mrs. Steadman to tell her that her Jack could not have killed a man from behind, and that he himself had declared that he had not done so. And it was all very well for Miss Unwin herself to feel convinced that Jack Steadman had not committed the crime of which an assize court had found him guilty, and for her three witnesses of character to back that belief. Yet the facts remained. And on the facts, she was soon to confirm, there seemed to be no arguing with that jury's verdict or the response of the Home Secretary to the appeal sent to him.

When she got back to the inn, she ensconced herself in Mrs. Steadman's neat-as-a-pin sitting-room and there read column after column, first of the local newspaper's account of the inquest, and then other accounts of the trial itself, which Mrs. Steadman had carefully pasted into the pages of an old account-book.

Evidence had been brought to show that there was no love
lost between the landlord of the Rising Sun and Alfred
Goode, who had come to Chipping Compton only some two
years before his death. There he had set up as a farrier, a
trade he had learnt as a cavalry trooper, and had rapidly
acquired a reputation for knowing much about the ills and
ailments of horses. But he had earned another reputation,
too, for charging high and working little. He had as well, the
prosecution had not troubled to deny, been widely disliked
for being foul-mouthed, ill-tempered, and frequently drunk.
More than once Jack Steadman had ordered him out of the
Rising Sun. But, out of malice, no doubt, he had persisted in
taking his evening beer in its taproom instead of at some
other hostelry. And he had spent much of his time there
making evil remarks about the landlord and the landlord's
wife.

Then there had been evidence that on the night of his
murder he had been good and drunk in the Sun. When Jack
Steadman had at last ordered him out, he had shouted from
the door, "I'm going now, but don't forget the night's not
over yet." And, finally, apart from the evidence of the
gamekeeper, who on his regular round had discovered those
two bodies in Hanger Wood, one dead, the other unconscious, there had been the evidence of the note found in Jack
Steadman's pocket, a note in Goode's vouched-for hand saying: *This must be settled once for all. If you think you can
bamboozle me, think again. Meet me at midnight in the
glade in Hanger Wood.*

And all Jack Steadman had had to say in his defence was
that he had not shot Alfred Goode, that he had not arranged
to meet him in Hanger Wood, that he had no idea how the
note had got into his pocket, and that he had no idea what it
meant.

He had protested and protested his innocence in this way,
with, it seemed to Miss Unwin, reading a little between the
lines of the long newspaper reports, a sort of fearful inno-

cence himself. He had not committed a murder. He would never have committed a murder. He would never have killed a man in the cowardly fashion in which Alfie Goode had been killed. And he had only to say that, loud and clear, to be believed of everyone.

But he had not been believed, and by this time a week hence he would have been two days hanged.

4

Miss Unwin had only just finished her reading of the newspaper reports pasted into Mrs. Steadman's old account-book when she heard thumping steps and the clink of dishes and cutlery outside the sitting-room. A moment later Vilkins cheerfully barged her way in with supper on a tray.

"Lawks, Unwin," she said, seeing the fat book with its pages flapping open, "you ain't read all that already?"

"Well, yes. I have."

Vilkins sighed. "It's a wonder to me 'ow you does it," she said. "An' me, what was a blessed babe along o' you, 'ardly able to make out more than the name of a pub above its door, if the letters is big enough."

"I was lucky, my dear, to have been placed in a household where the mistress was willing for me to share sometimes in what her own little girl was learning. You know, it all started there."

"An' look where it's finishing, with you a-solving mysteries what were baffling the 'ole o' the blinking police force."

"Now, Vilkins, I did not do that."

"Oh, yes, you did. That time when they suspected you of murder an' 'igh an' mighty Mr. Superintendent Heavitree was all set to send you to the Bailey, you soon showed 'im the rights an' wrongs."

"Vilkins, it was a lucky stroke only. Or little more than that. I had the advantage of seeing it all from a different point of view."

"Then what about that other time, when that Mr. Richard was so spoony on—"

"Vilkins. Not another word."

"All right, all right. I was only tellin' you what you knows very well for yourself."

"But I don't, my dear. Let me tell you something, something that you will hardly want to hear."

"What's that, then?"

"Simply, my dear, that I have read every one of these newspaper accounts and I cannot see any gap in all the evidence they say was brought against Mr. Steadman. Not the least gap."

Vilkins's face did fall as she heard this. "But, Unwin," she said, "you're the only one as could."

"And there's little more, I fear, that I can do now. One thing only I am sure about."

"That Jack Steadman didn't never do it?"

"Well, that, yes. But one small step beyond, too."

"Well, step it out for a girl, for 'eaven's sake."

"It's just this: If you look at the whole matter as it were upside-down, you see at once one certain thing."

"Upside-down? 'Ave I got to stand on me blinkin' 'ead then?"

"No. No, my dear. You have got to—or rather *I* have got to —turn the whole affair top to bottom in my mind. One must start by saying, not what everyone else has declared, that Jack Steadman must be guilty, but by saying no, if one thing is certain it is that Jack Steadman did not kill Alfred Goode. Then one thing is clear."

"It ain't to me," said Vilkins.

"No? Well, I shall tell you. It is that not only must someone else have killed Alfred Goode, but that that person went to great lengths to make sure that Jack Steadman would die, too."

"But 'e ain't dead."

"Not today he isn't. But by next Friday morning he will be. Unless I can find—unless you and I, Vilkins dear—can find who is that person who wished both Alfred Goode and Jack

Steadman out of the way. Unless we can find who that is, and prove it."

"Yeh," said Vilkins. She stood in thought for a moment, sturdy feet planted wide apart. "Yeh. Well, Unwin, you'll 'ave to do the thinking. That's for certain. I ain't up to it. Not by a mile. So you eat your supper, an' I'll get on with 'elping Mrs. Steadman, which is something what I can do and what she needs, poor soul."

So Vilkins clumped out, and Miss Unwin turned her attention to the chop and the potatoes and the fresh bluey-green sea-kale that awaited her. But she found she had little appetite.

Then, wanting something to drink, she took up the jug of ale Vilkins had brought on the tray, only to find she had forgotten to add a glass.

There was a bell on the table, a little brass shepherdess under whose ample skirt a clapper lurked. But Miss Unwin did not want to demand service at a time when the Rising Sun was in such difficulties. So she set out to see if she could find a tumbler without troubling anybody.

And just as she got down to the foot of the stairs, she saw stepping in at the wide door, fully illuminated by the still strong daylight of July, an unmistakable figure.

It was that of a man she had not known for a very long period. But when she had had dealings with him, they had been so vital to her well-being, to her life even, that his face, his bearing, and everything about him had been impressed on her mind for ever.

Had she encountered him in a London street, as she might have expected possibly to happen, she would have had no hesitation in taking the first turning she could so as to avoid coming face-to-face with him. But his appearance here, miles and miles from the metropolis, was so astonishing to her that before she could stop herself, she came out with his name.

"Mr. Superintendent Heavitree."

He looked up at the sound of her voice, and it was at once apparent that he, too, had recognised her.

"Miss Unwin. Good gracious me. What on earth brings you to these parts?"

Miss Unwin stepped off the last tread of the stairs and advanced a little along the passageway. Now that she had met the man who once had tried to persuade her to confess to a murder she had not committed, she was not going to show any fear of him, nor any dislike.

"Why, Mr. Superintendent," she answered, "I might ask the same question of you. What on earth brings you to the town of Chipping Compton?"

Her adversary of old looked little different from the comfortable tweed-clad yet disconcertingly shrewd figure she had known, beyond having replaced the waistcoat with the heavy watch-chain across it, which she had once had to contemplate across a police-cell table, with one in shepherd's plaid without a watch-chain. He gave her now a friendly smile.

"Your question is easily enough answered," he said. "I am here because I am no longer Mr. Superintendent, but only plain Mr. Heavitree, retired from the Metropolitan Police and all its cares, and living with my sister in a little cottage not two miles from here."

"So you are not visiting the town in connection with the murder the landlord here is supposed to have committed? I had not really supposed you were, indeed. The matter is considered closed by one and all."

Mr. Heavitree, lately Superintendent, gave her one of the swift, calculating glances she remembered well as emerging from his bluffly genial exterior.

"You do not seem quite to share that universal opinion, Miss Unwin," he said. "Any more than once upon a time you shared the opinion of us all that you were a murderess."

"You are right, sir. I do not share that opinion. But do I

gather that you are acquainted with the facts of the matter and believe like all the rest that Mr. Steadman is guilty?"

"Well, Miss Unwin, I will not disguise from you that, the affair having taken place almost on my doorstep as you might say, I did interest myself in it a little. I attended the inquest and I read some accounts of the trial."

"And you agree with the verdict there?"

"Yes. Yes, I have to say it. I think I hardly ever saw evidence so strong."

"But you have been to this house before? You know Mr. Steadman?"

"Why, no. No, I did not know him, and, as it so happens, I have never set foot here till this moment. But this evening I had some business in the town for my sister, and feeling thirsty I thought I would step in here, forgetting indeed that this was the inn where that murderer was landlord. It is, if I say it, a most extraordinary kind of coincidence that we two should have met again in this way."

"Yes, sir. Yes, it is," Miss Unwin said.

And a thought that owed nothing to that logical side of her mind abruptly entered her head then. A wild thought owing much more to mysterious intuition.

"Mr. Heavitree," she said, "might I ask a particular favour of you?"

"I owe you a great deal, Miss Unwin, as you know."

"Then may I ask you to spare some few minutes to meet Jack Steadman's wife? To meet her, to ask her about that business, and to tell me afterwards whether you still believe Mr. Steadman is a murderer."

Ex-Superintendent Heavitree looked plainly astonished. For several seconds he stood where he was, blank-faced.

"I have said, Miss Unwin," he pronounced at last, "that I owed you much. But I must confess I did not expect to be asked to do what you have asked me by way of a favour. Yet ask you have, and I will do as you wish."

So, after all, Miss Unwin did find Mrs. Steadman to beg a

glass to drink her ale out of. And while she was doing so, she asked if she would speak in private to the former Scotland Yard detective.

Upstairs, she ate the rest of her supper and drank her beer while the interview was taking place below. Cold and a little greasy though the remains of her chop had become, she forced herself to consume it to the last morsel. Somehow she felt that if she did what was her duty over that, the outcome of the talk she had arranged so much on the spur of the moment would be favourable.

But all the same, with the logical part of her mind she doubted that it could be. Mr. Heavitree was not a person to be won over by impressions, and it was only an impression after all that had converted her to Mrs. Steadman's cause. The evidence, the hard evidence, was all against. And it had been evidence that Superintendent Heavitree had dealt in all his working life, and would not be able to prevent himself from dealing in still.

Then at last the door of the sitting-room was opened by Vilkins, who poked her head in and spoke in a decidedly huffy manner.

"Mrs. Steadman asked me to show this gentleman up," she said, putting fearful emphasis on the word *gentleman*.

"Yes. Yes, thank you, my dear. You recognised him, I suppose?"

"And I recognised her," Mr. Heavitree said. "The young hussy who got herself locked up in your place in a police cell while you went and solved a murder case."

But he spoke with a smile, and Vilkins melted.

Before she had time to comment, however, Miss Unwin burst out with the question she had waited to hear answered all the while that she had masticated the cold remains of her chop.

"Mr. Heavitree, what do you think?"

The former detective officer stood looking down at her as

she sat at the table in the middle of the neat little sitting-room.

"I would never have thought it of myself," he said at last. "I never would. But, yes, Miss Unwin, I believe that dear good creature. She tells me her husband could not have shot that man because the shot came from behind, and here am I, a seasoned old police officer who thought he'd learnt never to trust a single soul, and I find that I believe that he never did."

Miss Unwin jumped from her chair and had to restrain herself from clasping her old adversary in a warm embrace.

"But what I believe and what I don't believe doesn't alter the facts, you know," Mr. Heavitree said. "Jack Steadman had Mr. Serjeant Busfield for him at the assizes, and in London Serjeant Busfield was an advocate we never liked to have against us up at the Old Bailey. He brings out the facts in favour to the very last drop, and always did."

Miss Unwin sank back onto her chair again. "Yes. Yes, I know how strong the defence was," she answered. "And how unsuccessful. But, Mr. Heavitree, there is one thing your belief, my belief, in Jack Steadman's innocence does alter. I was saying as much to my friend here not an hour ago."

"And that is what?"

"That once you begin to look at the matter from the point of view of Jack Steadman's not being the murderer of Alfred Goode, you see the situation in a very different light."

"To tell the truth, my dear, I have hardly begun to do that as yet. But, yes. Yes, now you say it, I see that if Mr. Steadman did not commit that terrible crime, then some other person must have."

"And there is something more," Miss Unwin said.

Mr. Heavitree thought for a moment. "Yes," he said again, "something more there is. Look at it in your way and it's plain that Jack Steadman has been set up, as we say, for this business. The murderer, whoever he is, could have killed Alfred Goode and left him so that no one could tell who had fired that shot. But he did more than that. Worse than that.

He arranged matters so that Steadman was bound to be suspected—suspected, tried, and hanged at the last. That blow to his head must not have been inflicted in an accidental fall."

"Quite right," Miss Unwin answered. "And another consideration came to me while you were talking with Mrs. Steadman."

"I shall be interested to hear any consideration you have had, my dear."

"Well, then, ask yourself, as I have asked myself, why this murderer should want to kill two men at the one time and, further, why he should have been content that one was to die instantly while the other was left to be killed—and that is what it must amount to—to be killed by the due process of the law."

"I see that you've a good question there," Mr. Heavitree replied slowly. "But I'm not at all sure I can see what answer there must be to it."

"An' no more can I," Vilkins said. "An', come to that, I ain't so sure as I understand the question."

"Well, let me tell you what I have thought," said Miss Unwin. "And then you can tell me what you think of my reasoning."

"Well, cough it up quick, do," Vilkins begged.

"It is this, then. Why should anyone wish to kill two men who were so different? The one a vicious drunkard, the other from all I have heard of him as fine a fellow as you could wish to meet? Well, I think the answer must be that each one knew in some measure some secret that the murderer wanted at all costs to stay a secret."

"Blackmail," said the former Scotland Yard man. "Yes, I dare say you've the right of it there, Miss Unwin, now I come to look at it. It is strange, very strange, that two men so different in almost every way should need to be murdered. When it was just a matter of Alfred Goode being done to death, why, then there were reasons enough, since from all that's been said he was plainly about as bad a lot as you could wish to find. But to want to kill both him and that decent chap Jack Steadman, well, blackmail seems your only answer."

"But there's more still," Miss Unwin said.

"More?"

"Yes, sir. Think. Surely blackmail, so you call it, must mean one other thing."

"It don't mean more to me than what it is," said Vilkins. "Just about the nastiest thing one 'ooman bein' can do to another."

"Yes, you're right, my dear. As always, when you speak from your heart. But this is what, perhaps, you have not thought of about that particular crime: that it means there must be a person who can be its victim, someone who has a secret worth money to the man levying the blackmail. And that means one thing more."

"A toff," said Mr. Heavitree. "A swell."

"Exactly. Someone who has something to lose, a great deal to lose, enough to make him break the Sixth Commandment in order to preserve his secret."

"The Sixth Commandment," Vilkins said. *"Thou shalt not kill.* I had that dunned into me at the end of the beadle's cane. Remember that, Unwin?"

"I remember."

"And I'll add yet another thing," Mr. Heavitree said, "though I dare say you've thought of it for yourself."

"That this toff of yours must be a toff from not very far away," Miss Unwin answered.

"That's it, my dear. From round about here, or otherwise the murder would not have happened in Hanger Wood."

"The Vally o' Death," said Vilkins. "An' now it's my turn to put in me pennyworth."

"Yes, my dear?"

"An' it's this: 'Ow are you going to nose out all the swells round about? 'Cos there's a good few of 'em, I'll tell you that. But, what's more, I'll give you your answer straightaway."

"But how, Vilkins dear? How can you answer that, which, yes, did puzzle me at once. How, in the terribly short time we have, can I go about seeing for myself all Alfie Goode's possible victims?"

"Simple," said Vilkins. "Easy as easy. Today's Sunday, all right? Well, tomorrow night as ever is up at the Hall there's General Pastell's annual ball, an' every single gentleman in the county'll be at it."

5

Miss Unwin's heart leapt up at Vilkins's announcement. As she had sat eating her gluey-cold supper, thinking over all she had learnt in her reading of the newspaper accounts of Jack Steadman's trial and fearing that ex-Superintendent Heavitree would never concur with her belief in his innocence, she had felt minute by minute an increasing despair. Yes, she did not waver by a hairsbreadth in her conviction that Jack Steadman had not killed Alfie Goode. But, as strongly, she thought of the appallingly short time there was before Jack Steadman was to be hanged. Four days only. Four short days.

But now, not only had Mr. Heavitree unexpectedly backed her, but there had been put before her a way in which she could at least get a glimpse of all the possible alternative suspects within the course of a single evening. Next evening.

She half began to think that she had been meant by a higher power to achieve the almost impossible task that faced her.

It was to Mr. Heavitree that she turned now.

"You have been frank enough to declare, sir, that you believe despite yourself in Jack Steadman's innocence," she said. "And you have done more. You have helped me to clear my mind about the true aspect of the affair. But I am going to ask you now a very great deal more. You know that?"

"My dear Miss Unwin," Mr. Heavitree said, "you do not have to ask. Here am I, supposedly enjoying a life of quiet retirement, but in truth fretting away with each day that dawns. No, the old warhorse scents battle. What I can do to help, I will. All day and every day."

"Thank you. I felt I could expect that answer. But to hear it spoken aloud gives me new hope."

Mr. Heavitree inclined his side-whiskered head in acknowledgement.

"Now, I'll tell you one practical step we might take," he said. "From what I have heard from Mrs. Steadman and what I recollect of the trial, there seems to me to have been one witness whose evidence was crucial."

"Arthur Burch," said Miss Unwin.

" 'Oo's 'e?" Vilkins asked.

"He, my girl," said Mr. Heavitree, "is a certain tenant farmer who was in this very house on the evening before the murder. In court he stated he heard Alfred Goode call out to Jack Steadman as he left here in his drunkenness some such words as *Don't you forget, you and I are to meet again tonight.*"

"No," said Miss Unwin. "That is nearly right, but I think the words were a little different."

Rapidly she turned the stiff leaves of Mrs. Steadman's pasted-in old account-book. She found what she wanted in a moment.

"Yes. Yes, look here. Two newspapers giving the same words: *I am going now. But do not you forget the night is not over yet.* Yes, that piece of evidence from Mr. Arthur Burch cannot but have told heavily."

"Well," Mr. Heavitree said, "I remember Arthur Burch at the inquest. He spoke up, and spoke up well. But something in his manner did give me at the time a moment's doubt. I put it down then to my own over-suspiciousness, the detective officer's vice. But if the evidence against Jack Steadman is to be challenged anywhere, there it'll have to be. So, as early as may be tomorrow—I must get home to my sister now or she'll be worrying—I shall do myself the honour of having a word with Mr. Burch."

"Thank you, my friend," Miss Unwin said. "I hardly think I myself would have much success there, not even in the guise I have already adopted of a lady magazine writer."

"Well, I dare say not. So I'll bid you good night, and I'll come here to tell you anything I can as soon as I learn it tomorrow."

Then, when the former detective had gone thudding down the inn's wooden stairs, Miss Unwin turned to her friend and helper of old. "Well, Vilkins dear," she said, "the ball that's to be held tomorrow night will give me a fine opportunity. But there is one problem still. How am I to gain entrance to the Hall to see it?"

"Yeh. I been thinking. An', Unwin, you're not going to like this."

"What am I not going to like? If I can help poor Mrs. Steadman, there will not be much I will baulk at."

"Not stepping downwards in the path what you gone up?"

"Stepping down?"

"Well, only a couple o' days ago Mrs. Perker, the 'ousekeeper at the Hall, was bemoanin' to me that she wouldn't 'ave enough 'elp for the evening of the ball. 'Where am I to get another lady's-maid from, Vilkins?' she said. 'Tell me that.'"

"A lady's-maid? Back to being a lady's-maid again?" Miss Unwin said.

She found the prospect plainly daunting. She had risen up from kitchen skivvy, rank by rank, in the house where she had been placed after her workhouse days till she had become indeed maid to the daughter of the family. But at last she had been encouraged to make the leap across that great barrier dividing gentlemen and ladies from the rest of the world and to become a governess. The distinction she had achieved was precious to her. Once beyond that barrier, the whole world lay open to her talents. Could she bring herself to go back down through it again, even if it was only for one night?

Yes. She must.

"If Mrs. Perker still wants an extra lady's-maid, my dear," she said to Vilkins, "I am willing to be that person, through and through."

"Then first thing tomorrow," said Vilkins, "you'd better go across to the Hall an' try your luck."

Miss Unwin, in a little pretty bedroom under the eaves of the Rising Sun, did not sleep well. She had too much on her mind.

Try as she might, she could not prevent herself every now and again, as she lay tossing and turning, from regretting her decision to play the lady's-maid. Alone in the dark, she was at times convinced that somehow, once a uniform was on her back again, she would never be able to get it off. Someone would assume that she had never been anything other than a maidservant, would order her imperiously to take service at some house or other in the neighbourhood, and she would be incapable of refusing.

When the thought became too oppressive, she sat up in bed and told herself roundly that it was nonsense.

But in another half hour, after lying there trying, for want of being able to get to sleep, to puzzle out who could possibly have played that devilish trick on honest Jack Steadman, she found that once again she was caught in the waking or half-wakeful nightmare. Condemned never again to live as a lady and to have those open opportunities before her.

She did sleep at last. But when she finally woke, with the noise of birdsong loud in her ears, she felt by no means ready to go and offer her temporary services over at the Hall.

Nevertheless, as soon as she had drunk a cup of tea and tried to eat a little bread and butter, she set off. As she strode out through the glittering morning air, over the three miles or so of softly dusty lanes, down the steep hill into the Valley of Death and half-way up the equally steep slope on the other side, she did her best to concoct a story about being a lady's-maid temporarily without a position who had heard of the housekeeper's difficulty.

But she found when, after some trouble, she came to confront Mrs. Perker, a thick-bodied lady in a stiffly pleated black satin gown, that the story she had patched together was scarcely good enough.

"Well, my good woman," Mrs. Perker said, "I hardly think I can take you into General Pastell's service even for the length of a day knowing nothing at all of you. The General, you understand, is a widower, and a great deal devolves upon myself."

"But I assure you, madam, I well understand the work."

Miss Unwin felt with bitterness as those words came to her lips how easily she had slipped back again into the subservient mode. But if she was to have the chance of observing the various gentlemen who might have been victims of the unsavoury Alfie Goode, then work as a maidservant in General Pastell's house that night she must. And take up again the respectful, even obsequious, tone of the good servant she must.

"I dare say you do understand your work, for aught I know," Mrs. Perker answered her. "But that is neither here nor there. You have told me scarcely anything of yourself, except that you cannot show me a letter of character. Why, you might be nothing but a wicked thief, or in league with a whole band of robbers, even. And I have a young child in the house, too, the General's granddaughter. No, I cannot take the responsibility."

For a moment Miss Unwin felt herself at a total check. But then the thought of Jack Steadman in the condemned cell came yet more vividly into her head, and of his wife, still bright-eyed and defiant but terribly in need of help. No, somehow she must get to see the gentry of the county. One of them, surely, had for some reason or another put himself at the mercy of the unscrupulous Alfie Goode and had at last taken a murderer's way out of his trouble. She must find him.

Otherwise Jack Steadman would have been hanged in his place by Friday.

But how could she persuade this obdurate woman to accept her services?

And then a notion came into her mind. A daring, even foolish notion, but one that had to be acted on at once if there was any chance of its succeeding.

She swallowed. "Mrs. Perker," she said, "there is something I have to tell you in confidence. In the strictest confidence."

"Now, it is no use you spinning me a tale, young woman. I want to hear nothing of a child without a father or any unpleasantness of that sort."

"No, no. The confidence I have to tell you of is not mine. It —it is, in fact, your master's."

"The General? What confidence can he have entrusted to you, a stranger, that he would not have entrusted to me, his housekeeper of twenty years?"

"Madam, it is simply this. You know that over in Chipping Compton the landlord of the Rising Sun inn, an old soldier in whom General Pastell has taken the keenest interest, has been accused of murder and found guilty?"

"Of course I know of the General's interest in the man. But that could have been a piece of mere gossip you picked up at the inn in half an hour. I expect you heard it from that chatterbox Vilkins who told you there was employment here."

"No, madam, I heard of it from the General himself. Or, to be more correct, my employer heard it from General Pastell and he passed it on to me. Madam, I am a female private inquiry agent."

Miss Unwin held her breath.

Mrs. Perker had only to go to the General and ask whether he had employed the services of such an agency as she had invented for her to be in much worse trouble than before. She might, of course, try then to persuade General Pastell all the same to use her services. But, much though he had tried to do on behalf of the former Corporal Steadman, it was in the highest degree unlikely that he would think there was anything to be gained now from the assistance, not even of an inquiry agent, but of a mere governess. She trusted, however, that the housekeeper would take her at her word.

"Let me explain a little," she added hastily. "General Pastell, as you must know, has from the start been most anxious to do all that he could to see Mr. Steadman acquitted, believing it was hardly possible for him to have committed so foul a deed. I do not know what assistance he gave to his defence in court, but some person must have paid for Mr. Serjeant Busfield's services, and then the General, as you will know, got up a petition when the verdict went against Mr. Steadman. But that, too, did no good. So as a last measure he has gone to the agency of which I am an employee."

"Yes, I understand that now. And, of course, it is not for me to question anything the General does."

At this, Miss Unwin took a little heart.

"But what I cannot altogether understand," the housekeeper went on, "is why, in the interests of Mr. Steadman, you should want to come here as a lady's-maid on the night of the ball."

"That is where I must beg you particularly to keep a confidence," Miss Unwin said.

She thought, in fact, that if she did succeed in convincing Mrs. Perker, it was not very likely that this particular confidence would be kept. To have in secret a private inquiry agent in the house—it was too good a piece of gossip to keep entirely to oneself. No, the news would spread. Like wildfire. But this was by no means a bad thing. If in the end it got to the ears of the man who had killed Alfie Goode and arranged for Jack Steadman to hang for it, then it might well stir him into some rash countermeasure that could cause him at last to betray himself.

It would be a countermeasure not without danger to herself. But for little, bright-cheeked Mrs. Steadman she would be happy to risk anything that had to be risked.

"I am sure I can keep a confidence as well as anybody," Mrs. Perker said.

Yes, thought Miss Unwin, and how many people can?

"Then I will tell you everything," she answered. "My employer has come to the conclusion that if Mr. Steadman did not commit the crime of which he was accused, then it is most likely that Alfred Goode was killed because he had learnt some secret and was asking too great a sum to keep it hidden. And, I regret to say, that the only persons susceptible of such a need for concealment are gentlemen who have reputations to lose. My employer considers that it is by no means unlikely therefore that the gentleman in question will be at the ball here tonight."

Mrs. Perker gasped.

And Miss Unwin knew then that she had finally earned her place as a lady's-maid when the ball should begin.

But would she, as she assisted the lady guests with their cloaks and mended perhaps a dress hem torn in the dance, be able to see something that gave her an inkling as to who had laid that terrible trap for Jack Steadman? And even if she did, would there then be time enough to produce proof that he and not the innkeeper had shot Alfie Goode?

6

When Miss Unwin returned to the Rising Sun from her interview with the housekeeper at Monkton Hall, she saw her new colleague, the former Scotland Yard detective officer, sitting at his ease in the private bar, a pint of ale in a pewter tankard on the oaken table in front of him. The very picture of a countryman of modest means dreamily whiling away the time.

But she had only to pass in front of the wide entrance door to the bar to see the tankard drained and the countryman get to his feet. She preceded him up the stairs to Mrs. Steadman's sitting-room, kept at her disposal.

Hardly had she taken off her bonnet when there came a quiet tap on the door she had left half open.

"Mr. Heavitree," she said, beckoning him in. "What news?"

The burly former superintendent stepped forward and closed the door carefully behind him.

"A little news, I think," he said.

"Do sit down and tell me quickly."

Mr. Heavitree settled onto a chair at the table.

"Don't expect me to tell you that I have caught out Mr. Arthur Burch in a flagrant falsehood," he said. "But on the other hand I am pretty well convinced that there was indeed a falsehood in that evidence of his."

"Then we are making progress," Miss Unwin said. "I did not dare to hope for any when I rashly undertook to see what could be done yesterday. But progress we have made, surely. If Arthur Burch was telling lies at the assizes, then he must have been doing so for a reason. He must have been paid or suborned to do what lay in his power to see that a rope went round Jack Steadman's neck."

"And," added Mr. Heavitree, "that payment, or that pressure brought to bear, must have come from the man who wishes to see Jack Steadman dead. That's true enough, Miss Unwin, and it is to you that I owe my certainty of it."

"But you were not able to obtain any hint as to who this man might be?"

"Oh, dear me, no. Dear me, no. I was far from that, I'm afraid. I presented myself to Mr. Burch at the cottage on his bit of a farm—and a pretty tumbledown place that is—I presented myself to him as a former police officer taking only the mildest interest in the matter, but somewhat curious nevertheless and happening to be passing near. And straightaway I could see that he did not like it."

"The former police officer? The hint of a threat?"

"Yes, that was the size of it. But I went about my way as hard as I could to reassure him, and I believe that by the time he consented to talk about the matter, he truly thought I was no more than an old buffer trying to warm the embers of a dying fire."

"Good. Well done. And what more did you learn other than those few words of evidence we read in Mrs. Steadman's newspaper extracts?"

"Little enough, little enough. In fact, I hardly think I heard anything more than the fact, or the so-called fact, we already knew, that he states he heard Alfred Goode call out to Jack Steadman, as the former left this place in a state of drunkenness, the words: *I'm going now. But don't you forget the night's not over yet.*"

Miss Unwin could not hide an expression of disappointment.

"Oh, but don't be too dismayed, my dear. I may not have induced Arthur Burch to budge from those words. But I heard him say them and repeat them three, four, or five times. And do you know? He repeated them like a parrot. Like a parrot every time."

"Yes," said Miss Unwin slowly. "Yes, no doubt you are right. If he was truly recollecting something he had heard three months ago, he would almost certainly have varied that speech, if only by a small hesitation here or there."

"And he did not," said Mr. Heavitree. "No, take my word for it as an officer who has questioned criminals by the score, by the hundred, in his time. That man had been drilled in what he was to say. Drilled and drilled till he had got it word-perfect. And I'll tell you something else."

"Yes?"

Mr. Heavitree pushed himself to his feet. "Come downstairs with me," he said, "and you can see with your own eyes what I mean."

"Very well," Miss Unwin answered, agog with curiosity.

She followed the ex-superintendent in his heavy progress down the inn's stairway. In the passage between the taproom and the private bar he stopped.

"Now, I don't know as you'll recollect," he said, "but it was given in evidence at the assizes that Arthur Burch was sitting that night as he always does in the private bar on my left here."

"Yes, I remember reading that."

"Good. And Alfie Goode, of course, had been getting drunk, as was his custom, in the taproom on my right here."

"Yes, I recall that too."

"Now, it was from behind the taproom bar that Jack Steadman at last ordered him out. That wasn't given in evidence, but it stands to reason that it must have been so. And I have taken the liberty already of confirming the fact from Mrs. Steadman."

"I will take your word for it. But—"

Mr. Heavitree held up a majestic hand. "No, hear me out. Now, we have Arthur Burch in the private bar and Alfie Goode leaving the taproom, there in its doorway just where you are yourself this minute, with Jack Steadman behind its bar barely five yards distant from him. Now, Jack Steadman denied in court that Alfie Goode had said anything about meeting him, did he not?"

"Yes. Yes, he was all but bound to do so, unless he wished almost directly to admit to the murder."

"Very well. Though he was not able to tell the court just what Alfie Goode did say, claiming in that innocent way of his that he couldn't remember a few trivial words, he was still nearer by a good few paces to Goode than was Burch sitting at the far end of the private bar there. Yet Burch swore and swore again to the exact words."

"Yes," said Miss Unwin. "Yes, yes, and yes again. He would have had more than a little difficulty in making out what Alfie Goode, doubtless in a slurred, drunken way, was saying. But he swore to the very words. Oh, why were you not advising the defence at the trial, Mr. Heavitree? It might have made all the difference."

Mr. Heavitree sighed. "It might have made some difference, I agree," he said. "But I think you're being too optimistic to say all the difference. And I beg you, Miss Unwin, not to start thinking we have only to telegraph this to the Home Secretary for a reprieve to be granted instanter."

"Yes," said Miss Unwin sadly. "Yes, I see that you are right."

"But take heart, do, my dear. We know something, remember. Something hard now. We know Arthur Burch is a liar."

"But does that advance matters after all?"

"No, not at present. But it does give us a way forward. A narrow and a difficult way, but a way nonetheless."

"Then let us take it, Mr. Heavitree. Whatever the difficulties."

Mr. Heavitree shook his head. "Not us, my dear, not us," he said. "You. You, Miss Unwin."

"Me? But I thought we had agreed Mr. Burch was your pigeon."

"Oh, yes. To begin with, he could not have been anything

else. When we needed quietly to find out what we could about the fellow, he would have told more to me than ever to a lady. But now we need to do something altogether different."

"Different? But what?"

"We need to frighten Master Burch, my dear. To frighten him to the very back of his teeth."

"So that he will tell us, not simply that he lied in the witness-box, but who it was that made him lie?"

"I always thought you knew one end of the stick from the other, Miss Unwin."

"Yes, that is all very well. Yet how are we to frighten the fellow? How am I to do it, since you seem to think this falls to my lot?"

"Ah, not altogether to your lot, no. To one of us after the other, I rather think."

"Then tell me what I myself must do."

"I think this. You must go to him, as soon as may be, in the guise you told me you have already once adopted, the lady writer from a magazine. You will not find it easy to persuade him to talk. But at least you must manage him in such a fashion that he does talk to you for a little, that he does answer some questions about his evidence at the assizes. You won't get him to modify by one jot those parrot words of his, but that won't matter. All you have to do is to make him remember the saying of those words in court, in short his abominable perjury, and to call to mind the man who forced him—how, we do not know—to commit that perjury."

"Yes," said Miss Unwin. "Yes, I can do that."

She almost rose from her chair and set off for Arthur Burch's farm that moment. But then she remembered her morning's work.

"Mr. Heavitree," shes said. "This is difficult indeed. You see, in order to have all the gentry of the county under my eye, I have persuaded the housekeeper at Monkton Hall to take me on for the evening of General Pastell's ball tonight as a lady's-maid. But she wants my services within the hour, and I think, going about the house with my fellow servants, I may well learn something that at least might be helpful to me tonight."

Mr. Heavitree sighed once more. "Then we shall have to wait till tomorrow to carry out what I may call the Burch side of our investigation," he said. "Time is pressing, of course. Three clear days only remain now. But it cannot be helped. Your going to the Hall may after all prove our best way forward. And perhaps, too, there's something to be said for letting Master Burch stew for a little. Yes, stew and worry, worry and stew. I rather like it."

Miss Unwin waited only to tell Vilkins, who was herself due to go back to the Hall for the busy evening ahead, that her plan had succeeded. Then she snatched a bite to eat and set out again for General Pastell's big house.

She found preparations for the ball in full swing.

Ahead of her as she trudged the last hundred yards up the hill to the tall iron gates she saw the men of the local band, their bandmaster chivvying them from the rear, their bright brass instruments dazzling in the rays of the sun, making their way to the house to rehearse. In the grounds, gardeners were going to the back doors with flowers by the barrowload. Two others had heaved from the ice-pit in the shadiest corner its last remaining enormous block of ice, shipped in winter from distant Norway. Protected from the sun now by layers of dampened sacking, in the cool of a pantry indoors it would be broken into pieces and used to chill champagne and make the ice-puddings without which any self-respecting ball would be considered a failure.

Indoors, Mrs. Perker, plainly harassed, received her with a quick command.

"Go to the servants' hall. Ask for Rosa, who was poor Mrs. Pastell's maid before she died. She will give you a dress that I trust will fit, and then, lady's-maid or no lady's-maid, you must help where you're wanted."

But after this she took a step nearer and dropped her voice. "And as to you-know-what, you must shift for yourself as best you can. And you may be sure I have not told a soul."

By which Miss Unwin knew that one soul at least must have been told. And that that one soul would tell another, and that other yet one more. If the man who had shot Alfie Goode was to be at the ball, it was more than likely that sooner or later he would learn that a female detective, one of those creatures more written about in sensation novels than active in real life, was there to spy on him. But fictional exaggerations might well stand her in good stead. The man she wanted to start from his lair might be all the more nervous because of them, and perhaps all the more ready to make a move. It would be a dangerous move for her, no doubt, but, if all went well, a fine false move.

She found almost at once that some of her guesses were correct. When she entered the servants' hall, more than one pair of eyes regarded her with more curiosity than a mere ordinary newcomer might expect. And when she was taken by Rosa to see if one of her crisply starched black cambric dresses would fit, she received final confirmation.

Rosa said nothing directly. A dress was found and a few stitches put in it to adjust the waist. Then, as Miss Unwin, now from head to foot a servant once more, was leaving the bedroom, Rosa ventured one quick remark.

"There now, miss, you'll be as fine a lady's-maid as myself."

The "miss" was the betrayal. Miss Unwin thanked her new fellow servant and ignored the tiny slip.

For the next few hours, in fact, she had little opportunity to think of how she had stepped down from governess to maid, and not much more chance, as it turned out, of working at the reason she had had for her descent. When "the whole county" is coming to a ball in a house in only a few hours, each and every servant in that house will be kept busy one way or another, from housekeeper of twenty years' service to lady's-maid just employed that day.

So Miss Unwin—plain Unwin now—made herself useful, and did no more than hope she might learn a little. She collected newly polished lamps from the lamp-room, with their wicks well trimmed, ready for the night's illumination in a country house as yet far from having the convenience of city gaslight. She took a fresh jar of beeswax to a pair of footmen dragging the gardener's boy on a polishing mat up and down the parquet of the ballroom. She fetched candles by the box to fit into the glittering chandeliers. She went to the still-room to take from its cupboards and long shelves preserves and liqueurs and put them where, when the supper hour came round, they would be needed. She even stepped outside once to the game-larder, isolated in its back courtyard where its rank odours would not be offensive, to bring well-hung birds to the kitchens.

She made sure, too, that she had everything she herself might want in the little morning parlour, where during the ball she was to sit and be ready to assist with hot tongs if careful curls had fallen from their place or with needle and thread if some minor repair was needed.

So, in the end, only once in all the hours of preparation did she find a moment to do something towards furthering the task she had undertaken. This was when, late on, she caught a glimpse of Vilkins, busy as herself. She managed to draw her aside.

"Dear," she said hurriedly, "you, too, can play your part tonight."

"What, me a female detective? You don't know 'oo you're a-talking to."

"Oh, yes, I do, my dear. To someone who has eyes in her head, and good sharp ones, too."

"Well, I won't say as 'ow I can't see what's in front o' me nose."

"And there are a good many good people who let themselves be blinded when it comes to that. So this is what I want you to do tonight. Simply look and listen. And if you see or hear anything that seems even a little out of place, let me know of it when you can."

"Out o' place?"

"Yes, just that. Because, unless I'm very much mistaken, there will be here tonight amidst all the festivities one man who will be out of place indeed. A murderer, my dear, no less."

"An' what've I got to look out for? Blood on 'is 'ands?"

Miss Unwin smiled. "No, nothing as plain as that, I'm afraid. But that man killed a villain not so many weeks ago, and, more to the point, he is even now hoping and praying that the law in its majesty will kill a good man for him before the week is out. So he may not manage to behave quite as he should. And perhaps, only perhaps, either you or I shall catch a glimpse of that 'not as he should.' "

"Then I'll keep me old peepers as peeled as peeled," said Vilkins. "Trust me for that."

7

Then at last there came the hour of the ball. Carriages rolled up to the wide-open door of the old house. Ladies in gowns of gauze and muslin were handed down from them. Gentlemen in evening dress stepped out afterwards. Gentlemen in evening dress or, Miss Unwin noted, watching discreetly from the doorway of the little morning-room where she was on duty, very often in military uniform, as might be expected when a general entertained.

It was at this time, too, that she got her first sight of General Pastell, standing at the back of his long entrance hall welcoming the guests. She was impressed, even deeply, by what she saw. The General was so plainly a soldier, for all that he was no longer of an age to be active. But the utter straightness of his back, the firm set of his shoulders, the rigour of his white moustaches, all proclaimed the military man even more than the glitteringly epauletted uniform he wore so proudly. Yet even from a distance it was plain that he radiated kindness and good humour. Each new guest appeared to be questioned about health and family and kept long enough for a full answer. And each one left him smiling.

Yes, Miss Unwin thought, I can well understand a man like that taking so much trouble to save a lowly soldier from the gallows. No wonder Mrs. Perker accepted at once that daring lie that he had employed a private inquiry agency even at this late hour. Why, it might be thought the old gentleman had some special reason for his kindness.

But she had no time now to speculate on the character of the man under whose roof she was working in secret. Lady guests began to flood into the morning-room to leave wraps and cloaks, and more than one needed help to repair some minor disaster to hair or complexion that had occurred on the journey to the Hall.

Eventually, however, the rush ended. The band Miss Unwin had followed up to the house earlier in the day could be heard from the ballroom blowing and scraping hard as they could go, and from elsewhere in the big house came the sound of conversations and laughter.

In the scurry of the arrivals, Miss Unwin had had little time to eavesdrop on what one lady was saying to another, though she thought that if some particularly scandalous subject had arisen, she would have caught it. But it was not likely, she reasoned, that the real gossip of the neighbourhood, which might give her a clue as to who could be a victim of Alfie Goode's extortion, would be broached at the start of the evening. Ladies not in the inner circle of county society must be present as well as those at the heart of affairs. So the latter would certainly be restrained—until two or three of them happened to be alone in the room together.

Just then the stately figure of Mrs. Perker, contriving somehow to be unobtrusive at the same time, came sailing in. There was no one else in the room, and the housekeeper at once placed herself within an inch or two of Miss Unwin's chair.

"I think I ought to tell you, miss," she murmured, though with no loss of dignity, "there has not been one single person invited tonight who has not appeared. I say no more. You will understand."

"Yes," Miss Unwin murmured back with gratitude. "I do indeed understand, madam. But—but I am somewhat hampered by not knowing the names of so many of the guests."

"I had thought of that," Mrs. Perker whispered. "Take this."

And from the bosom of her dress, embellished for the evening with a brooch of garnets, she took a long sheet of paper, thrust it into Miss Unwin's hand, and at once glided away in a swish of black satin.

Miss Unwin looked at the sheet. It was the housekeeper's own carefully written-out list of all the guests, their names and styles. If the man she had to find was in truth a member of county society, then his name was surely here and he himself was dancing to the *rum-tum-tum* beat of the music in the ballroom or sitting somewhere in conversation.

But, dancing in cotillion or quadrille or tucked away in talk as he might be, how could she get so much as a look at him? Let alone catch him, whoever he was, by some lucky chance appearing more preoccupied than a reveller should be? Or— and this was perhaps a little more likely, she thought—making discreet advances to a lady not his wife?

She decided that she had to risk deserting her post for a little and go quietly here and there about the house as if busy on some errand. Perhaps she would catch a glimpse of someone behaving in the way she had described to Vilkins. A gentleman in the library, where the butler presided over a table set with silver pails of champagne on ice, drinking to excess? She might be lucky.

But, glance this way and that as she would, she saw nothing in any way out of the ordinary, and the minutes went ticking and ticking by.

A feeling of depression began to cling round her like a heavy mist. All that she had gone through to get herself here at this heaven-sent time, and was she going to have nothing to show for it?

Then, having stayed away from her post a good deal longer than was wise, as she made her way back she did have a single stroke of luck. It was not a matter of seeing a dancer looking as if he would rather be anywhere than in the whirl of a lively galop. Nor was it the sight of some secret toper. Nor of a yet more secret lover amid the banks of ferns and hothouse plants in the conservatory.

It was simply overhearing one man talking with another as

she hurried past the open doorway of the small room on the outside of the house specially fitted up for gentlemen to smoke in.

"Yes," she just caught the words, "a damned female detective. I had it from Miss Troughton, who heard it from one of the maids."

She came to a halt, looked left and right to see if she was observed, and, finding the coast clear, sidled nearer the open door.

"Some nonsensical idea of General Pastell's," she heard the voice resume. "Something to do with this fellow they're hanging."

"Oh, yes, I know. Old soldier."

"I dare say. But to have a spy in the house, and a female one, too. It's not what I call decent."

"I suppose not."

"No, by God, it ain't. I tell you, if I knew which the wench was, I'd take a whip to her."

Miss Unwin, half hidden behind a bust of the Duke of Wellington standing on a sturdy pedestal of purple porphyry, began furiously to wonder.

Was this savage response to her presence that piece of out-of-place behaviour she was looking for? It was not absolutely certain. But she must get a look at someone who was so much put out by the thought of a female detective watching him.

Cautiously, she put her head round the stern bust of the victor of Waterloo. The two talkers had their backs to the door, sitting side by side on a cushioned bench flanked by two stuffed foxhounds. Cigar smoke was wreathing up from between them.

"Yes, by God, a whip."

The man who uttered the threat was an officer in uniform. Miss Unwin even recognised the regiment. It was a truly famous one, illustrated in the Rev. C. P. Wilkinson's book. The 13th Hussars, heroes of the Charge of the Light Brigade

itself, though the man who so objected to her presence was a
captain too young to have taken part in that glorious affair.

"My dear Brackham," she heard his companion remon-
strate, "let old Pastell act as he thinks fit. He is a hero, after
all."

"A hero, I dare say. But that's a deuced odd thing to do."

She dared wait no longer. Either of the two smokers might
turn his head at any moment. Or in the morning-room an
impatient lady might be waiting for attention.

But she had learnt perhaps enough. Captain Brackham. Of
the 13th Hussars. A possible suspect. Yes, surely a possible
suspect.

And, mercifully, the morning-room, when she got back to
it, was deserted. No long skirt had had a clumsy foot tear it in
the dance. No elegant coiffure had succumbed to the energy
of a waltz.

She sank down on her little chair behind the long table and
breathed more easily.

She would give a good deal to know more about Captain
Brackham. But, if he was no more than a bully unduly concerned with his dignity, was there perhaps some other officer
or other gentleman visitor who would want to use more
violent methods on the secret interloper?

Barely had the thought entered her mind when from
somewhere in the room behind her she heard a noise. In the
room she had thought to be deserted.

She darted a glance at the door. She had left it only just
ajar, and she herself on her chair in the far corner must be out
of sight of any passer-by. Between her and that means of
escape lay the room's whole width, as well as the obstacle of
the long table in front of her.

Where had that sound come from? It had been too distinct
to be caused by a puff of breeze through the curtained window or even the scurry of a mouse in the wainscot.

She sat, glued to her chair, and tried to identify the direction of the sound. The room now, certainly, was utterly quiet. Deathly quiet.

And, yes, she thought after a little, the sound had come from behind the heavy dull red curtains across the window.

She slowly turned her head and peered towards them. There seemed to be no sign of anybody lurking behind them waiting to strike. But, she remembered from when she had drawn the curtains herself, the window protruded a foot or so from the wall outside, leaving a space where anyone could stand unobserved.

What should she do?

Should she try getting to her feet, darting round the table and making for the door? But to do so would be certain to alert whoever was behind the curtains. He would leap out and could easily get between herself and the door. And then? Perhaps, if it was indeed Alfie Goode's murderer lurking there, would he hesitate over killing again?

She almost felt strong, unyielding hands round her throat.

Then, on the point of making up her mind on a dash for safety after all, there came from behind the thick curtains another sound.

A sneeze.

And somehow it seemed to her at once that whoever was hidden there could not be any real danger. Someone who could sneeze? And, having sneezed, stay still?

In half a dozen rapid strides, she was at the window. She seized the two halves of the curtains with both hands and flung them wide.

Standing, back pressed against the darkened panes of the big window, hands spread to either side as if sheer wishing could cause the glass behind mysteriously to melt, was a girl of about twelve or thirteen. Miss Unwin saw at once that, though the Scotch plaid day-dress she wore was buttoned askew and though she was without stockings, she was a young lady.

Then she remembered a remark Mrs. Perker had made

while she had been desperately attempting to gain employment. She had complained that besides her other responsibilities she had a child to consider, General Pastell's granddaughter.

This must be she. The knowledge at once put Miss Unwin back into her state of governess-ship.

"What on earth are you doing hiding here?" she said. "You ought to be in bed, you naughty child."

The girl gradually relaxed her stance against the dark window. She stepped forward beyond the curtain and gave Miss Unwin a steady, half-insolent look.

"I'm meant to be in bed," she said, "but I came creeping down to watch you."

"To watch me?"

At the thought, Miss Unwin recollected her disguise as the lady's-maid who had been taken on for this one night.

She gave herself a mental shake, dropping the upright attitude of the indignant governess and assuming the pose of a servant.

"But why should you want to come and watch me, sitting here taking the ladies' cloaks and wraps and maybe doing a bit o' mending?" she asked.

The girl gave a loud laugh. "You can't fool me," she said cheerfully. "You look awfully like a lady's-maid, I grant. But I know better."

She knows I am a governess, Miss Unwin thought, feeling a wave of shame at being caught, as it were, out of the station she had taken such pains to attain.

"And that's why I came creeping down, of course," her captive went on with a touch of scorn. "I'm never going to get the chance of seeing a real female detective at work again, however long I live. So I wasn't going to miss this."

Miss Unwin had had time to think now, time to adjust herself again.

"Well," she said, "you're a clever one and no mistake.

You're the General's granddaughter, ain't you? What's your name?"

To Miss Unwin's surprise, General Pastell's granddaughter blushed.

"It's beastly Euphemia," she said. "How any parent could be so cruel as to land a girl with Euphemia beats me. And then to go off to India half the time."

"So are you called Euphemia? Or something else?"

"Well, it's Phemy usually. But I'd be plain Jane, if I ever had my way."

"Well," Miss Unwin said with a smile, "I think I had better be content with Phemy if, as I hope, we're to become better acquainted."

"You mean you'll let a fellow stay? And can I watch you trap the murderer? Do you have a weapon hidden somewhere about you? Is it a life-preserver? And what is a life-preserver? I've always wanted to know."

"Well, that's no more than a little club, and I'm sorry to tell you that I carry nothing of the sort."

Miss Unwin, the memory of Captain Brackham's threat returning to her, and the thought of an even more menacing threat that might await if the Captain was not the man she had alerted to the presence of a female detective, so-called, rather wished then that she did have somewhere about her person just such a weapon. But it was an idle regret.

"No, Phemy," she said, "you won't be able to watch me strike anyone down with a life-preserver. But there is, perhaps, something you can do for me. I suspect you're a girl who keeps her wits about her."

"I jolly well hope I do. You have to if you're stuck with a name like Euphemia."

"Good, then. So what I want you to do is to tell me about some of the guests here tonight."

"So you can find out which is the wicked murderer?"

"Yes," Miss Unwin admitted wryly. "For that reason, more or less."

"Right-ho then, Fire away."

For a moment Miss Unwin was tempted to resume her role of governess and to point out to General Pastell's granddaughter that there was a ladylike way of speaking. But she had more urgent matters on her mind.

"Well, now," she began, "what about Captain Brackham? Do you know him? Do you know anything about him?"

"I should jolly well say I do. He's the most terrible fellow for being fast, even though he's got no more brains than I have in my boot. He gambles most fearfully, and you should see the way he takes his fences out hunting. I wish I had a horse like his Caspar. Only I'm not allowed to hunt till I'm fourteen."

"He's fast, you say?" Miss Unwin asked, wondering how right it was to ask a child like this for further details.

But a man's life was at stake, and she did not regret having put her question.

The answer she got showed her quickly enough that her fears had been groundless.

"Fast? You should see him with that beastly Mrs. De Lyall."

"Mrs. De Lyall? I don't think I've heard of her. Is she at the ball tonight?"

"Ain't she just. You couldn't keep her away. Not that poor Grandpapa much wants to, if you ask me."

Miss Unwin decided to pass over this too intimate detail of family life.

"Describe Mrs. De Lyall to me then," she said.

"Oh, you can't have missed her. They say she's half Spanish, and no one seems to know whether there's a Mr. De Lyall or not. He don't come down to Oxfordshire, that's for sure."

"Yes, but what does Mrs. De Lyall look like? What sort of a dress is she wearing?"

"The red-and-black, of course. The one that makes her look like a Spanish dancer. Why, I bet she does her *cachucha* dance before the night's out. She always will, if she's let. She knows it draws the gentlemen's eyes, and all's fish that comes to that one's net."

Again Miss Unwin, the governess, wanted to issue a rebuke. But again Miss Unwin, the female detective, kept her thoughts to herself.

"I know that lady now," she said. "I remarked on that dress when she left her cloak. She has those very dark ringlets, has she not? And a high complexion?"

"And a high reputation," Phemy chimed in. "Why, she does things and says things that no other lady in the county would dare."

"Come, how do you know that?"

"Oh, I've heard Grandpapa say it many a time. And his great friend and rival, General Bickerstaffe, too. It's about as much of a case of smite with him, if you ask me."

"But you say that no other lady in the county behaves like Mrs. De Lyall?" Miss Unwin asked eagerly, an idea blossoming in her head.

"No, not a whit."

"Then you have already been more than a little helpful to me," she said to Phemy.

It was true, she thought. If it so happened that there was only one lady in the whole neighbourhood who was such a cause of scandal, then it was likely, surely, that her own task had been immensely lessened. If Alfie Goode had been killed because he was extorting money from somebody, was it not more than likely that that somebody was a lover of Mrs. De Lyall's?

No doubt, of lovers or would-be lovers she would have a fair number, but at least the circle of possibilities seemed to have been made sharply smaller.

Only, how was Jack Steadman involved? What could he know, and not know that he knew, which had made it imperative for Alfie Goode's killer to get rid of him, too, by the slow process of the law?

However, that was something she would have to think

about when she had time. At present she had more urgent matters in front of her.

"How can I get to see Mrs. De Lyall?" she asked rapidly. "To watch her and the men who speak to her and flirt with her?"

But before her young helper could answer, from just outside there came the sound of hasty steps.

8

The door of the morning-room was tentatively rattled.

"Quick," Miss Unwin whispered to Phemy, "back behind the curtains."

Hardly had Phemy whisked the curtains across her hiding place than the door was opened and a lady of a certain age wearing a gown in apple-green brocade came in.

"Oh, I have got the headache so badly," she said. "Can you find me a composing draught, my girl?"

"Yes, madam," Miss Unwin answered at once, every bit the well-trained servant. "It won't take me a minute. Will you lie on the sofa here? And I have some eau-de-Cologne just by me."

She handed the lady a handkerchief soaked in the eau-de-Cologne and hurried away.

She was not quite happy to do so. What if Phemy sneezed again? But there was nothing else to be done, and she suspected now that the first sneeze Phemy had let out had in any case been designed to draw attention rather than the other way about.

It did not take her long to get to the still-room, where she knew a quantity of a laudanum preparation had been left in readiness. Carrying a small glass of it on a tray, she quickly made her way back.

The lady seemed not to have been disturbed. She was lying where Miss Unwin had left her with her eyes shut and the soaked handkerchief spread over her pale forehead.

"This should help you feel better, madam," Miss Unwin said.

The lady sat up and drank down her draught. But then, to Miss Unwin's intense irritation, she closed her eyes again and lay back.

Would it be right to creep from the room and leave her where she was? And would it be safe to beckon Phemy from behind the curtains to follow? She must get to know as soon as possible if there was anywhere from which she could observe the notorious Mrs. De Lyall and the men who hung about her.

She decided to give the ailing lady just five minutes by the ormolu clock on the room's mantelpiece before risking signalling to Phemy. And her decision proved justified. The clock's gilt minute-hand had moved forward for only four of the five minutes when the lady abruptly sat up, declared she felt a little better, and said she would go and look for her husband.

Hardly was she out of the room when Phemy burst through the curtains.

"Hey, miss," she said, "you know who that was, don't you?"

"No. No, who was it?"

"Why, only the wife of your deadly rival."

"My rival? What do you mean?"

"Don't you twig? That's Mrs. Major Charteris, and her husband's our new Chief Constable."

"Oh, is the county Chief Constable here?" Miss Unwin said coolly. "I suppose he would be, if all the gentry of the neighbourhood are invited. But why do you call him my rival?"

"Well, I should think that's plain. I'm beginning to wonder whether you're much of a female detective after all."

Miss Unwin thought quickly. She must regain her slipping reputation with this child. The imp was such a find as a source of knowledge.

"Ah, you mean that the Chief Constable was responsible for Jack Steadman's arrest, and I am here to find him innocent?"

"Hit it right away."

"Well, that's as may be. But what I want now is a good chance of observing Mrs. De Lyall while I myself remain unseen."

"Pooh, that's easy."

"Easy?"

"Yes, there's a little gallery above the ballroom. Grandpapa told me once that when the ballroom was the great hall of the house, musicians used to play there. But it'd come tumbling down now if you tried to get all our band up into it, great fatties that they are."

Once more, sharp words about personal remarks came into the head of Miss Unwin, governess. And once more Miss Unwin, detective, silenced them.

"Then lead me to your gallery," she said. "Quickly, before anyone else comes and complains of the headache."

"I can't," Phemy answered.

"What do you mean, you can't? Listen, child, it is vitally important for me to set up a watch on Mrs. De Lyall. A man's life may depend on it."

Her fierceness did have the effect of wiping the grin off Phemy's face.

"Oh, miss," she said, "don't be cross. I only meant I'll have to tell you how to get to the gallery because I can't come with you. Grandpapa's awfully kind-hearted, but if he saw me going about the house dressed as I am, no stockings and everything, there'd be a most fearful row. He'd have an apoplexy on the spot."

"Yes, of course, you're quite right. You go back and hide where you were, but tell me first how to get to the gallery."

Phemy's instructions were complicated. But Miss Unwin forced herself to memorise them exactly. It was, truly, vital that she should be able to observe Mrs. De Lyall and, more important even, to watch the men who buzzed round this female honeypot.

In the end she found, hurrying through the house keeping respectfully close to the walls, that her young helper's directions had been needlessly involved. Within two minutes she was opening a small door in an upper passage. And then, to her quick satisfaction, she saw beneath her the brightly lit floor of the ballroom and heard coming up in bouncing waves of sound the music of the band, playing on a dais just underneath.

The gallery, she found, was conveniently shrouded in darkness and, needing only to untie the white apron at her waist, in her black cambric dress she could count on being invisible to anyone chancing to look upwards, even if she put herself at its very edge.

For a little while she watched the lines and circles of the dancers, forming and re-forming below, the swirl of spreading tulle skirts, the glint of jewels in hair and on bosoms, the white dazzle of starched shirt-fronts, the bright kaleidoscope of coloured uniforms. Nowhere could she spy, however, the bold red-and-black dress she remembered having seen when the lady guests had taken off cloaks and mantles.

What if Mrs. De Lyall was not dancing? She might well have declined and gone instead for some refreshment, accompanied, no doubt, by a male escort. And who would that be? And would his mere presence at the lady's side be any proof that he was her secret lover and the murderer of Alfie Goode? Or would Mrs. De Lyall be in the conservatory? Was she there at this moment seated behind an enshrouding bank of thick-growing ferns, allowing someone a furtive embrace?

The cheerful music of a cotillion came to an end. The dancers dispersed.

But then into the middle of the empty floor there stepped a figure Miss Unwin recognised, even seeing only the top of his head. General Pastell.

"Ladies and gentlemen, fellow officers," he said in parade-ground tones. "I am happy to tell you that I have just succeeded in persuading our good friend, Mrs. De Lyall, to dance for us her celebrated version of the famous Spanish *cachucha.*"

There was a loud murmur of appreciation, with, Miss Unwin thought, more in it of masculine growl than feminine squeak.

Then the bold black-and-red dress she had looked for so keenly suddenly emerged on to the bare floor below. No doubt the General's "persuasion" had taken place in some quiet corner, away from prying eyes. The band began to play, not very comfortably, a rhythmical, Spanish-sounding tune.

Mrs. De Lyall stood, head lowered, in the very middle of the floor, attentively waiting. And out of the surrounding circle of onlookers there came stepping towards her none other than Captain Brackham. He was carrying in front of himself a red velvet-covered box. He went up to the waiting danseuse and, with a military click of heels, held the box out to her. She opened it and took out what Miss Unwin recognised, from some illustration in a book for her young charges somewhere, as a pair of black castanets. In a moment she had them fastened round her wrists. Captain Brackham withdrew, and the lady began to dance.

Even seeing the performance from high above, it was plain to Miss Unwin that it was an altogether exciting affair. Whatever other qualities Mrs. De Lyall possessed, she certainly had dash. Watching her fling herself boldly backwards, arms above her head, castanets furiously clicking, two things became increasingly plain. The first was that the lady was clearly overstepping the bounds of feminine decorum, and the second was that almost all the gentlemen in the surrounding circle of onlookers were delighted that she should do so.

But was one of them more delighted than any of the others? Was Captain Brackham, who had been allowed to offer her the box of castanets, more favoured than the rest?

The music rose to a climax. Mrs. De Lyall swayed and swung till, from above, her wide red-and-black skirt looked like a shimmering circle of fire. And then, with a final *"olé,"* the wild dance came to an end.

There was a storm of applause.

When at last it began to die down, General Pastell stepped forward to escort the dancer away. But he was not allowed to reach her.

Another figure came smartly out of the throng, a man of much the same age as the General.

"Gad, no, Pastell," Miss Unwin heard his voice ring out. "You fellows of the Light Brigade have had more than your share of our dear friend's charms this evening. It's the turn of the boys of the Heavy Brigade now."

The stout, middle-aged man marched bravely up to the exhausted dancer. "Madam, may I have the honour of taking you in to supper?"

"General Bickerstaffe," came Mrs. De Lyall's voice, tinged with just a hint of Spanishness, "I should be delighted."

General Bickerstaffe, Miss Unwin said to herself. General Bickerstaffe, of the Heavy Brigade, those brave soldiers of the Crimea who had had their full glory dashed from them when the Light Brigade had made its blunder-led charge into the Valley of Death. Is he the man I am looking for, after all?

And it was true, she thought, that someone as comparatively aged and as socially respected as a general would be a great deal more likely to be Alfie Goode's victim than someone younger and perhaps unmarried.

She decided that, if the supper hour had come, she had better get back to her post in the morning-room.

There she found that her services were much in demand. A good many ladies wished to make themselves more presentable before taking supper. For the best part of twenty minutes, she did not have a moment to think of her own affairs.

At the back of her mind, she hoped Phemy Pastell was still

in her hiding-place, and had the sense to do nothing that would give herself away while the room was occupied.

But at last the rush abated, and soon there were only two rather elderly ladies standing in front of the cheval glass put into the room for their use, each politely offering it to the other as they chatted.

"My dear, such an exhibition."

"Yes, my dear. Disgusting is, I think, the *mot juste.*"

"Indeed it is. And it was not that dance alone."

"No, indeed. There was afterwards."

"Poor Bickerstaffe is plainly besotted, my dear."

"Yes. Yes. Such a pity. Such a brave man. Such a reputation."

"Yes, indeed, although I must say that I never approved of that absurd rivalry of his with dear General Pastell. Why men can never talk to each other without wishing to quarrel like two barnyard cocks is more than I can imagine."

"I am afraid your farmyard allusion is not far from the truth in this case, my dear. If you ask me, that woman is at the root of the whole rivalry."

"But don't you think that Captain Brackham . . . ? I understand he is staying at the Fox and Hounds, not a hundred yards from her door, and is in her house from earliest morning till late at night."

"If it is not the other way round, my dear."

"Oh. Oh. Do you think so?"

"Well, I certainly heard through my maid, who seems to know one of General Pastell's keepers rather better than she ought, that a person has been seen making his way through the De Lyall gardens at a very early hour."

"Oh, my dear. Every day?"

"No. No, to tell the truth, I gather that this was some months ago and that it has ceased to happen recently. If what my Elmore says is at all correct."

"But Captain Brackham was at the Fox and Hounds at that time?"

"History does not relate, my dear."

And the two tittle-tattlers left the morning-room, oblivious of the discreet presence of a lady's-maid in its far corner.

As soon as the door was shut behind them, Miss Unwin hurried over to the window and its heavy curtains.

"Phemy," she whispered, "are you there?"

"Aren't I just?" said Phemy, stepping out into the room. "And didn't we just hear something?"

Miss Unwin longed to administer a rebuke. But the need to have the opinion of an expert on the revelations that had just come out was too strong.

"Do you think it was all more than just gossip?" she asked.

"Oh, yes, it was. Much more. I know Lady Horrocks's maid, Elmore. She's being courted by Grandpapa's under-keeper, who talks to me like anything when there's nobody by. So I expect it's all true as true."

"And Captain Brackham is the man in the garden? You're sure?"

"Well, why else would he want to stay at the Fox and Hounds? It's the worst inn for miles round. Everyone says so."

"Then I have a good deal to think about," Miss Unwin said.

"Are you going to denounce him?" Phemy asked, eyes bright. "Will you go right up to Major Charteris, the *great* Major Charteris, Victoria Cross, tell him that he and his merry men are quite wrong, and then unmask Captain Brackham as the real murderer?"

Miss Unwin smiled, despite her underlying concern. "Oh, if it were as easy as that," she said. "But first I have got to find proof, hard and firm proof. Just going to the Chief Constable and announcing who I believe the real murderer is would never do."

"No. Perhaps you're right. Old Charteris is a fearful Tartar."

Miss Unwin's heart sank. She had hardly considered as yet how exactly she was to bring the affair to an end, so far from even guessing at a solution had she felt herself. But now, when at last an active possibility had come to light, she contemplated with more than a little dismay the need to inform the fiery Major Charteris. After all, she, a mere governess, would have to convince the head of the county police that the efforts of his own men, in which he doubtless took pride, had been entirely misguided.

How would she do it? How *could* she do it? But she must. She must if Jack Steadman was not to be hanged in a little more now than four days.

And Jack Steadman himself, how did he fit into all this? How?

9

Miss Unwin was soon to feel she had an even stronger reason for going to Major Charteris and claiming he had been wrong to have Jack Steadman arrested, and this was to make her yet more perplexed about how she could tell him what she would have to without arousing the Tartar in him, which Phemy Pastell had spoken of with such relish.

As the ball came to its end, it was only the thought that she could not yet be certain in naming Captain Brackham as the true murderer that gave her some comfort. It was at least an excuse to put off the evil moment. There was always, after all, General Bickerstaffe still to be considered. Certainly a general would be a more likely victim of blackmail than a mere captain.

She wished she had had an opportunity of finding out more about General Pastell's rival. But Phemy, when at last there had come a chance to talk to her safe from disturbance, had been overcome by such a tremendous fit of yawning that she had not had the heart to press her. Nor did she think a girl three parts asleep would be much help. Perhaps next day there would be an opportunity to see her again.

"Now, miss," she said, "it's high time you were getting back to your bed. You've been really helpful to me, but I don't see there's more you can do now."

"Have I really helped?" Phemy asked, stifling yet another yawn. "Helped a real female detective? I'll keep your secret, I promise, but I'll be jolly proud in my heart of hearts as long as I live."

With that, she seemed content to leave. She slipped open

the window behind the red curtain, assured Miss Unwin that she could get back to her own room by the servants' stairs "easy as a fish," and vanished into the darkness.

General Pastell had, with a thoughtfulness Miss Unwin had not been surprised to learn of him, made sure that a groom with a dogcart was there when all the guests had gone to take herself and Vilkins back to the Rising Sun.

Settling down beside her friend in the starlit darkness, she asked herself whether the long night had been worthwhile.

Yes, it certainly had. Before it, she had not had a single name in her head as a possible murderer. Now she had at least two.

But a moment later a new element was added to the scarcely sorted facts in her mind.

"Unwin," Vilkins whispered as soon as they had set off.

She felt on her cheek the little shower of spittle that had always accompanied Vilkins's whisperings, even when they had been helpless children together.

"Yes, dear?"

"I got somethink to tell. Important."

"Then tell."

"Can't."

Vilkins jerked her head back with immense significance towards the groom sitting sleepily watching the pony trot his way along the familiar lane.

Miss Unwin nodded agreement to this silence, though she suspected that anyone sitting back-to-back with herself and Vilkins could hardly overhear whispered words. Nor could she help wondering, a little disloyally, whether when they arrived at the Rising Sun Vilkins's revelation would not turn out to be a damp squib.

But it did not.

No sooner had the groom wheeled the dogcart round and set off again for the Hall than Vilkins seized her by the arm.

"Unwin," she said. "Guess what I heard."

"My dear, just tell me. I long to get to bed. I am altogether exhausted."

"Ah, but this is important. What you call vital."

"Well, then?"

"I was doing what you said, Unwin. Going about where I 'ad to, keeping me lug-holes well open. An' it was a good thing I did."

"Yes?"

Waves of tiredness pounded through Miss Unwin's head. Bed, bed, bed, she thought.

"Well, I'd been sent to take a glass o' lemonade to a lady what was in the conservatory, an' all of a sudden I 'eard voices."

"Voices? Whose?"

"That Mrs. De Lyall was one. You couldn't never mistake 'er, sort o' foreign-sounding as she is."

Miss Unwin's tiredness melted away. "And the other?" she asked.

"Well, is there a gentleman name o' something like Bash'em? Capting Bash'em?"

"Captain Brackham? Is it Captain Brackham?"

"Yeh, yeh. That's it."

"You heard Captain Brackham talking with Mrs. De Lyall? And saying something that seemed important?"

"Oh, it was important, all right. No question."

"Then what was it, Vilkins dear? What was it?"

"Well, it was like this, see. I was taking that lady 'er lemonade, an' you knows we 'as to take it on a salver, silver salver. Well, I don't know as 'ow anyone manages to carry anything on one o' them slippery things. Why, you can't just take the glass in your 'and and—"

"Vilkins!"

"All right, all right. I'm coming to it. Well, it so 'appens as I spilt a bit o' the lemonade. Couldn't 'elp it. So I stops to give that there salver a bit of a wipe with me apron. An' where I stops, just inside the conservatory, is where one o' them little windows is a bit open, it being the warm night it is."

"And you heard something through it?"

"Clever monkey. Yes, I did. I heard that Spanishy lady say, 'No, no, I knows you're worried,' an' the chap as was with 'er sort o' growled a reply that 'e was not. But she goes on an' says it again, an' louder. An' then 'e says to 'er, '*Sssh.*' But she says, '*It's all right, there's no one to 'ear.*' An' 'e repeats, still growly-like, that there ain't nothink amiss. Then this is what she says, an' I give it to you gospel true. She says: '*It's that female detective. You're worried by 'er, aren't you? Worried sick, I know it.*' An' 'e mutters, '*Damn you,*' something or other, an' off 'e goes, crunch, crunch, crunch on the gravel o' the path. An' a moment later into the conservatory comes that Capting Bash'em, so I knows as it was 'im she was a-talking to. Now, that's important, Unwin, ain't it? Ain't it?"

"Yes," Miss Unwin said. "It is important, very important."

But, overwhelmed with tiredness once more, all she could do was to say a quick good night, take the bed-candle left out for her, and almost stagger up to her bedroom.

Within minutes she was sleeping as deeply as ever she had.

She woke at her usual early hour, however. For a few minutes she lay where she was, looking dazedly at the clear morning light pouring in through the thin cotton curtain of the little low window and listening to the chorus of birdsong outside.

Then she began to think.

Three days now. Three full days only before Jack Steadman would be taken from the condemned cell and marched to the waiting gallows. And what had she achieved in her fight to save him? Something. Yes, in justice to herself she must admit that something had been achieved. By firmly taking the view that Jack Steadman was not guilty, she, with the unexpected assistance of Mr. Heavitree, had at least raised the clear possibility that someone else was responsible for the death of Alfie Goode.

But that was only the first step along the way. What lay next was the harder task of proving herself right to the satisfaction of the Chief Constable, whose men had seized on the easy option of arresting Jack Steadman when he had been so obviously left as the murderer. She had to show Major Charteris that someone else had not only murdered Alfie Goode but had deliberately made it look as if his killer was Jack Steadman.

And she was still far from achieving that, unless what Mr. Heavitree had found out about the lying witness, Farmer Burch, could be made to lead to the truth. Unless she herself could in the course of the day ahead frighten Arthur Burch into confessing who had persuaded him to give his false evidence. Would it prove to be Captain Brackham, as seemed most likely after what Vilkins had overheard at the ball? Or was it perhaps, after all, General Bickerstaffe, about whom she knew so little? Or was it even someone else?

She thrust aside the bedclothes and got up.

Little more than an hour later, she was marching, cotton parasol in hand, along the narrow, dust-thick lane leading to Arthur Burch's isolated cottage among the green open fields sloping steeply down the sides of the Valley of Death. She had dressed herself with care, despite the shortness of time. If she wanted her quarry to believe he was speaking to a lady magazine writer, it was essential that she look the part.

Fearing that, in this lonely spot, she might already be under observation from an upper window in the ugly little square-built stone cottage she could see at the lane's end, she began peering about her this way and that as if the countryside was something unfamiliar to a lady from London.

A cow on the far side of the hedge suddenly gave a low moo, and, delighted with the chance, she put on a show of starting back in dismay and then scurrying by on the opposite side of the lane.

Soon she had arrived at the gate to the patch of ill-kept garden surrounding the cottage. She opened it and, passing by a scatter of garments draped on a bush to dry and looking as if they had been left there all night, approached the door. A heavy, rust-covered iron knocker embellished it. She lifted it with difficulty and brought it tapping down politely.

She had to wait much longer than she had counted on before she heard heavy steps inside, and the passing minutes took from her much of the assurance she had set out with.

At last the door was creakingly opened by the man she recognised from Mr. Heavitree's description as Arthur Burch. He was not an attractive person. His clothes were old and bore plain traces of the farmwork that brought him his meagre living. His round, sullen-looking face was unshaven and his thatch of dark hair uncombed.

In a moment the rank smell of sweat assailed her nostrils. She swallowed. "Good morning," she said with all the brightness she could muster. "I trust I have not called too soon in the day, but I imagine countryfolk are early risers."

"What d'you want?" Arthur Burch grunted, seemingly by no means impressed by this show of sweetness and light.

Miss Unwin gave a small ladylike cough. "My name is Shaw," she said. "Miss Henrietta Shaw, and I represent the *Englishwoman's Domestic Magazine.* My editress, Lady Bolsover"—the invention had come to her in a flash—"has commissioned me to come to Chipping Compton to write an article on the effects of a murder on those connected with the affair. And I am approaching you, as one of the principal witnesses at the trial of that dreadful man Steadman, to ask if I may have your impressions."

"You cannot."

But Miss Unwin had been prepared for a rebuff at the start. She drew in a breath. "Now, Mr. Burch," she said, "perhaps you do not realise that I am empowered by Lady Bolsover to make some payment to any persons willing to give me their valuable time. I am sure that a farmer like yourself

has many calls upon him, so of course the compensation I
would offer would be correspondingly large."

"How much?"

Miss Unwin was left at a loss. Though she had thought on
her way to the cottage that she might have to dangle a re-
ward, she had not at all considered figures.

"That would depend," she replied quickly, "on what you
have to tell me." Then, raising her closed parasol till its point
seemed to be directed at the farmer's legs, she spoke more
sharply. "Had we not better go inside?"

Arthur Burch backed away a pace, and Miss Unwin
stepped across the threshold.

Quickly she looked about. The passage onto which the
door of the cottage opened led only to a flight of dark stairs.
To left and right there were doors, the one on the right wide
open, leading into a gloomy kitchen where on a large deal
table a scatter of dirty dishes could be seen. The door on the
left was open only by two or three inches, and as the farmer
saw her glancing towards it, he stepped forward till he nearly
pushed himself into her and closed it with a bang. Miss Unwin got just a glimpse inside. But she thought the bed she saw
was hung with curtains a good deal cleaner and fresher than
anything else in the neglected-looking house.

So, did Arthur Burch have richer tastes than seemed
likely? And, she asked herself, did that mean he needed more
money than his small tenant farm brought him?

"You'd best step into the kitchen," he grunted now. "It's
none so tidy. But my old mother's all I've got to look after me,
and she's failing."

"I quite understand, Mr. Burch," Miss Unwin answered,
doing her best to twitter. "So sad when our dear parents
begin to show the passing of the years."

She looked round the kitchen, which was decidedly lacking in tidiness, and spotted a chair that seemed rather more
clean than any of the others. Hastily she sat herself on it by
way of making sure of her right to stay.

"Well, now," she said, "I believe that it was you, Mr. Burch, who had the dreadful task of giving the most telling evidence against that man at the assizes."

"I don't know about that," Arthur Burch answered surlily.

"Well," Miss Unwin said, inventing hastily again, "I had the privilege before I came down to Chipping Compton of hearing the opinion on the trial of a very devoted friend of Lady Bolsover's, the eminent Queen's Counsel, Mr. Lionel Gathergate. And he was quite clear that it must have been your evidence that was decisive."

"I only said what I had to."

"Well, yes, of course. But that must have been a dreadful experience for you, to realise that on your word alone a man might hang."

Arthur Burch's dark, unshaven face took on a look of smouldering rage. "That's a damned lie," he said.

Miss Unwin did her best to look like a lady trembling with the offensiveness of that "damned."

"I really think, Mr. Burch," she gasped, "that you should not doubt the word of a lawyer as eminent as Mr. Gathercole."

"Gathercole? Gather*cole?* You said his name were Gather-*gate.* A damned odd sort of a name, I thought."

"Why, why, yes, I did. It is Gathergate," Miss Unwin replied, contriving some agitated movements of her hands. "I cannot think why I should have said Gather*cole.* One makes these mistakes, you know. Silly though they are."

"I dare say."

Miss Unwin breathed more easily.

"Well, I was asking: Did you not feel dreadful when you came to give your evidence?"

Was this what Mr. Heavitree would have wanted of her? He had said that the more Arthur Burch was made to dwell on his lies, the better. But was she going too far?

Certainly the farmer did not seem happy. He was standing and shuffling from one mud-smeared foot to the other.

"Dreadful?" he said at last. "I don't see why you say that. I spoke the truth, you know. I spoke the truth."

"I'm sure you did, Mr. Burch. I'm sure you did. But what I would like to know, for the purposes of the article I am writing, you understand, is: What were your feelings as you spoke that truth?"

"Feelings? I don't know as I go in for feelings."

"But you must have felt something. Something, when the thought came to you that a man, perhaps an innocent man, was going to be hanged on your word alone."

"Innocent? What do you mean, 'innocent'?" Arthur Burch was shouting now. He cast a furious glance round and suddenly darted off towards a far corner of the gloomy room.

What was he doing? Had she now gone too far at last?

The answer came a moment later. From the darkest corner of the dark, cluttered room Arthur Burch had snatched a shotgun. And now it was pointing directly at herself.

10

Miss Unwin looked at the shotgun aimed squarely at her and at the glowering man behind it.

"Mr. Burch," she said, "don't be silly."

She put all the command she could into the words. No use now in playing the twittering lady writer. Only a show of absolute confidence would save her, much as in very different circumstances her governess's authority quelled rebellion in the schoolroom.

For several long seconds the barrel of the gun stayed unwaveringly pointing. Then, slowly, it was lowered.

"Mr. Burch," Miss Unwin said, firmly as before, "if you do not wish to speak of your evidence at the assizes, you have no need to do so. There are others in Chipping Compton who can supply me with the impressions I require for my article."

"Well, I'm damned if I'll supply you with mine," Arthur Burch growled.

Miss Unwin rose from her chair. "Then I will bid you good day," she said, "and we will regard this incident as closed."

She turned, not without an inward fear that Arthur Burch's shotgun might not stay lowered, and left the crowded and cluttered kitchen.

A moment afterwards she was out in the bright morning sunshine again. With the stout door of the cottage safely behind her, she found herself trembling uncontrollably from head to foot.

But she dared not linger so near the scene of that threat to her life, and, forcing her melting legs to obey her, she set off back up the long narrow lane leading from the ill-kept farm.

Not until she had reached the great oak-tree that marked the turning did her trembling cease.

When at last Miss Unwin got back to the Rising Sun, Mrs. Steadman came down the stairs towards her. With a shock she saw how one more long night had affected the bright-eyed soldier's wife. Her ramrod uprightness had yielded at last to a definite stoop, and her crab-apple cheeks were blotched with paleness.

But still she kept her dignity.

"Good morning, my dear," she said. "You were out be-times."

No shadow of a hopeful inquiry about what progress might have been made. Miss Unwin wished with all her heart that she had something good to tell. But she hardly had, and she was not going to give Jack Steadman's wife false hope.

"Mrs. Steadman," she said, "I have been out on the business I came here for, you may be sure of that. But, sorry though I am for it, I cannot bring you any good news."

"No. Well, if back in May Inspector Whatmough in all his experience couldn't do better than arrest my Jack, I shan't expect no miracle from you now, my dear."

Miss Unwin sighed. "Oh, a miracle is needed, I'm afraid," she answered. "Three days is a terribly short time. But if anything can be done to make a miracle happen, then I promise you I shall do it. And Mr. Heavitree, too. I know I can speak for him."

"You can speak *to* him, too, my dear. He's been sitting in my room upstairs this half hour waiting for you."

So Miss Unwin hurried away. She did not feel she had learnt anything in her morning's frightening visit to Arthur Burch, but it had confirmed, surely, that he was a deeply worried man. She would welcome the former detective's response to that.

In the sitting-room Mr. Heavitree lumbered up from the sofa where he appeared to have been having a quiet doze.

"Well, Miss Unwin," he said, "I gather you were out early. It was to Farmer Burch's?"

"Yes, of course."

She told him in detail then all that she had seen at the cottage and what had happened to her there.

"Yes," he said when she had finished, "we've got Master Burch well scared, no doubt of that. So it only remains to complete the little business I had in mind for him."

"To complete it, Mr. Heavitree?"

"Yes," said the old detective cheerfully. "If I'm any judge, what that fellow needs now is a good shock. And that I propose to give him. Only it must wait, I fear, till this evening."

"But what is it?"

"Why, simple enough. I want him to find that the bumbling old police officer he met yesterday and the not very effective lady writer he frightened off this morning are, in fact, fast friends."

"Yes. Yes, I see that to discover the two of us together would be a shock indeed to him. But why must we wait till tonight?"

"Ah, because the shock will be all the more effective for being unexpected. I want Master Burch to come innocently to this very house to drink a pint or two of ale, as I hear he still does despite everything nearly every blessed evening of his life. And here I want him suddenly to see the pair of us in earnest conference."

"Yes. I understand the merits of that. But it will lose us— what?—eight or nine hours. Eight or nine precious hours, Mr. Heavitree."

"Yes, I like that no more than you, especially as there's little to be done in the meantime, so far as I can see. But if we're to get Arthur Burch really quaking in his boots, we'll have to take every advantage we can. So wait we must."

"Is there nothing to be done in the meanwhile?"

"Well, one thing I do mean to do, and that's to keep an eye on our fellow. He may get to thinking about the risk of what he did at the assizes and then wonder about that former police officer, bumbling though he seemed."

"And make a bolt for it?"

"Exactly. But if he does, I shall be after him. And when I catch him he'll break, all right."

"Good," said Miss Unwin. "And there is something I think I should do this morning."

"Oh, yes?"

Then she told her colleague what she had seen and learnt at the ball.

"So I want to know all there is to be known about General Bickerstaffe," she concluded. "And I think I know the best source to go to."

"Your naughty little friend, Miss Euphemia Pastell?"

"Her."

Mr. Heavitree rose to his feet. "Well, each of us to what we can do best," he said, "and let's pray we meet with more success than we deserve."

Miss Unwin was about to wish him equal luck when something that had been in the back of her mind all last evening made her stop.

"Mr. Heavitree, one last thing before you go."

"Yes, Miss Unwin?"

"It is this: I can quite easily see why someone who was having an illicit affair with Mrs. De Lyall and who wished to keep it secret might be made Alfie Goode's victim and so might need in the end to murder him. But . . ."

"Yes, my dear?"

"What I cannot see is how that person would need also to end Mr. Steadman's life in the way he plans to. How can it be that Mr. Steadman knows something about a murderer which yet allows that murderer to risk letting him stay alive till Friday morning?"

Mr. Heavitree sat back down on the sofa again. "Yes," he said, "that needs a bit of thinking about."

For some moments he sat in silence contemplating his

large brown boots. Then he sighed. "You know, my dear," he said, "I think it must mean that perhaps we're barking up the wrong tree."

"Yes," said Miss Unwin, who had been standing contemplating her neat black shoes, dusty from her walk. "Yes, I too begin to think there may be another tree, that perhaps it is another sort of secret altogether that Alfie Goode found out about. Yet if Mrs. De Lyall was not what he was able to exercise his blackmail over, what else could it be?"

"What indeed? But it may be so. However, I suppose for the present you can do no better than find out what you can about General Bickerstaffe, and I shall certainly keep a watch on Master Burch. Remember this: He must know who persuaded him to give false evidence against Jack Steadman, and with luck and patience we can find that out, too."

So, shortly after Mr. Heavitree had set out to keep watch on the perjured tenant farmer, Miss Unwin left the Rising Sun once more. She went with no great feelings of optimism. Only three days now till the morning Jack Steadman was to be hanged, and all she could do by way of saving him, it seemed, was to gossip with a thirteen-year-old hoyden.

But she had hardly gone fifty yards from the inn when her attention was attracted by the sound of horses' hooves clattering out loud and fast on the road ahead. A moment later round the next bend there came at a fast trot a truly magnificent canary-yellow phaeton, two splendid roans in its shafts, a burly coachman in the driving seat, and two footmen, tall and statue-still in their cocked hats and frogged coats, behind.

Who on earth can be driving such a magnificent equipage in this quiet little country town? Miss Unwin asked herself.

In a moment she realised that she might have guessed the answer. As the open carriage came nearer, she recognised, under a flower-bedizened bonnet and despite a thick veil, Mrs. De Lyall.

Now, where can that lady be going in such a hurry? Miss Unwin asked herself again. Her senses prickled with alertness. Could it be something to do with Jack Steadman? Was this hurried journey some consequence of the conversation Vilkins had overheard?

But to her surprise the carriage, instead of hurrying on towards the inn and beyond, came to an abrupt halt almost at her side, its broad-chested horses rearing and stamping.

And then her surprise was redoubled.

Mrs. De Lyall threw back her veil and called out in a loud, imperious voice, "You! You there, miss! I want to talk to you."

Miss Unwin looked all round her. But there was no one else in the sun-drenched quiet road to whom Mrs. De Lyall could possibly be speaking.

Cautiously she approached the shining yellow phaeton.

"Come nearer, come nearer. Do you think I want every peasant in this wretched place to hear my private affairs?"

Miss Unwin stepped right up to the door of the carriage. Mrs. De Lyall looked down at her.

"Now, my fine miss," she said, "I have just one thing to tell you. And that is this: Unless I hear that you have left this place before nightfall today, I shall know how to make you go."

It took Miss Unwin a moment to recover from the shock of this. But it was a moment only.

"Madam," she said, "I do not think we have been introduced, and I quite fail to understand what it is that you are talking about."

"I am talking about you, you nasty spy," Mrs. De Lyall answered. "Don't think that just because you come down here to poke and pry, others cannot make their inquiries, too. I heard at General Pastell's ball last night that there was a female detective somewhere about, and I have made it my business since to find out who it is and where she was to be found."

"And to come and order me out of the town?" Miss Unwin

asked, inwardly sinking at the swiftness of Mrs. De Lyall's action but outwardly treating her with unswerving calm.

"Yes," Mrs. De Lyall answered, her high cheekbones reddening with rage. "Exactly that, my fine miss. To order you out of the town, out of the county. And if you have any ideas about not doing as you're told, I suggest you give the men behind my carriage a good look. They may be dressed in coloured coats and white breeches with wigs on their heads, but let me assure you they can do a man's business when there's need for it."

Miss Unwin managed to prevent herself glancing at the two impassive footmen up behind the phaeton. She had had a good look at them already, and knew them for six-footers.

"Madam," she said to Mrs. De Lyall, striving to keep the calm in her voice still, "I acknowledge that I am here to make inquiries relating to the murder of Alfred Goode, but I fail altogether to see what interest you may have in the matter."

"That is none of your business, my girl. Just take heed of what I have said to you. If you are still in the town by nightfall, you can expect some rough handling. That's all. Coachman, drive on."

The coachman, who had sat listening impassively to all of this, lifted his whip—higher than was necessary, Miss Unwin thought—and brought it cracking down on the flank of one of Mrs. De Lyall's splendid roans. The phaeton jerked forward, and in a minute the dust from its wheels was rising up in a cloud in Miss Unwin's face.

She stepped back into the shade of one of the cottages fronting the road and waited for her heart to beat less furiously.

Then she began to consider.

The first thought that came to her was that she had no intention whatsoever of leaving Chipping Compton. Not while there was any chance of saving Jack Steadman from the rope. Then she thought, with a certain savage pleasure, that the morning had plainly advanced matters towards sav-

ing him, after all. Because if Mrs. De Lyall had gone to the
length of threatening her in that way, then she must be a
worried woman. Or be closely connected with a worried
man.

But who was that man? Was it Captain Brackham, staying
at the wretched inn at the gates of her mansion? Or was it
perhaps General Bickerstaffe, who had so much more to lose?
Or was it someone else she had yet to connect with the lady?

But, whatever the answer, there now seemed a great deal
more point in finding out all she could about the Heavy
Brigade general.

And there was something else.

Turning, Miss Unwin retraced her steps to the Rising Sun,
deep in thought.

There she went round to the back and, as she had hoped,
found Vilkins, her arms deep in a wooden tub of soapy water.

"Well," Vilkins greeted her at once, "you got any further?"

"Yes," said Miss Unwin. "Yes, I think that quite unexpectedly I have."

"What you found out then? Not who really murdered Alf
Goode?"

"No, not that. Not yet. But I have found out that whoever it
is seems to be so worried by what Mr. Heavitree and I have
done so far that they have begged Mrs. De Lyall to drive
down here on purpose to threaten to have me beaten by her
footmen unless I leave the town before tonight."

"An' you're going?"

"What do you think, my dear?"

"Well, so you're staying. But I should keep your 'ead well
under cover if I was you. I've 'eard tales about them two, an'
they weren't such nice tales neither."

"Yes. Yes, I suppose I had better be careful. But I have done
more than be warned off, you know. I've had an idea as well."

"An' it's a good 'un?"

"I hope so. I can't quite think what put it into my head. But it was something to do with Mrs. De Lyall just now and the men I saw last night buzzing round that over-rich honeypot."

" 'Oneypot? I'd call 'er a sight worse nor that."

"Well, that's as may be. But one thing struck me about those gentlemen."

"An' what's that?"

"You can't guess?"

"Never saw most of 'em, did I? So I ain't got nothink to say."

"No, you're right. Well, I'll tell you. They were all military men. And, much farther down the social pyramid, so once was Mr. Steadman. Well, now, it struck me that in their past in the Army some of those guests at the ball might have been in the same campaign or at the same camp or something of the sort as Mr. Steadman."

"An' that's where 'e might of got to know somethink about one of 'em without realising it, like?"

"Now, that is clever of you, my dear."

"Oh, I got me 'ead screwed on all right, even if it does look a bit funny."

"But I wonder if you can guess what I want you to do about this idea of mine?"

Vilkins lifted a soapy hand and scratched vigorously at her frilled cap. "Can't," she said.

"Well, I want you to go up to London and make inquiries at the War Office."

"Eh? You gone out o' your mind?"

"No, dear, I don't think I have. You see, we're in a hurry, a deadly hurry. If we weren't, I might try taking this idea of mine to the Chief Constable and trying to persuade him that it was his duty at least to explore the possibility. But I should never succeed in doing that in the few days we have left."

"I should say you wouldn't. I've 'eard about that Major Charteris. Regular fire-eater 'e is."

"Yes, I have heard as much, too. But if there is no chance of going to the top at the War Office—and that institution wears altogether too much of a thick brass helmet on its head to pay any attention to a mere governess—there is still what you might call the soft underside."

"Clerks," said Vilkins.

"Clerks indeed, my dear. Clerks who go for a drink after they have finished their copying duties for the day, or who go out at their lunch hour. Clerks who'll talk to a girl who knows how to be friendly."

"Which," said Vilkins, "is yours truly."

She put her hands behind her back and untied the strings of her big sacking apron.

11

It did not take Vilkins long to put a few clothes into a basket while Miss Unwin went to Mrs. Steadman and explained why she was going to deprive her of the help General Pastell had so kindly sent to her. The two of them reached the station in good time for the midday train to London.

On the platform, Miss Unwin gave her deputy investigator final instructions.

"Vilkins, dear, are you sure you can remember every name on that list?"

She had handed Vilkins the list of names that the housekeeper at the Hall had given her and had carefully read it to her three times over.

"Oh, yes, Unwin. I'll remember, don't you fret. Not knowing 'ow to read's a great 'elp, you know. An' besides, I *can* read, a bit."

"Well, if you are sure . . ."

Miss Unwin thought that, despite her friend's somewhat muddled logic, there was a good deal of truth in what she had said. People who could not read often had remarkable memories. Vilkins was quite likely to have been able to commit to mind all the names and ranks of the officers who had attended General Pastell's ball. Among them, since "the whole county" had been invited, there ought to be the man who had killed Alfie Goode and would have killed Jack Steadman on Friday morning.

"And you'll do it all as quickly as ever you can?"

"I told you already, didn't I? I don't want to see poor Mrs.

Steadman the morning 'er Jack's topped, no more than what
you do."

"Yes, yes. You're quite right, dear. It's only that time is so
short, and I hate having to put such a difficult task into your
hands. But I cannot leave Chipping Compton. Mr. Heavitree
and I have to play out our comedy with Arthur Burch tonight."

"No, I knows that, Unwin, and you can trust— Oh, gor-
blimey! 'Ere's the blessed train."

Round a curve in the gleaming rails there came, snorting
and grinding, the express that in the space of less than two
hours would take Vilkins to the metropolis and her meetings
with copying clerks from the War Office.

"Goodbye, dear. Goodbye and the best of luck," Miss Unwin said as the steam monster came to a halt.

She bundled Vilkins into a third-class carriage—she had
offered her a second-class ticket, but Vilkins would have none
of it—and saw her safely place her basket on the rack above
her seat. The station porter came along the platform cheerfully banging closed any open doors. The train guard blew his
whistle and waved his green flag. The wheels of the long
express began slowly to turn, and the great monster was off
on its journey.

When it comes back, Miss Unwin thought, will it bring
Vilkins triumphant with some link between Corporal Jack
Steadman and one of the military gentlemen at General Pastell's ball? Will she find one? Or will she have to return
defeated?

She herself left the station and set off at once down into the
valley in the direction of the Hall. Perhaps there was nothing
to be gained from finding out about General Pastell's great
rival, General Bickerstaffe. But she must not leave anything
undone that might lead to the hard evidence that would free
Jack Steadman. Phemy Pastell's gossip was the best opening
still left to her.

She pondered, as she made her way along between the

dense banks of white-headed cow parsley on either side of the lane, how she was going to get to see Phemy. After the ball had ended, she had been given the wages due to her and had been in two minds about accepting money for work she had hated having to go back to doing.

So she had no excuse for presenting herself at the Hall a second time. There was even some risk of having Mrs. Perker discover that General Pastell was not, after all, the person who had employed the services of a phantom inquiry agency.

But when she got to the gates she saw that her worry had been needless. Some twenty yards inside the grounds with their expanse of trim lawns there was a cedar of Lebanon, a huge spreading tree, dark green and still in the hot midday air. And, perched on one of its thick branches some fifteen feet above the ground, happily chewing at an apple and swinging her legs with scant regard for ladylike deportment, was Miss Euphemia Pastell.

Miss Unwin waved her parasol.

"Half a min'," Phemy yelled.

The apple core described a graceful parabola in the air. Phemy rose to her feet, launched herself, caught hold of a branch some five feet farther down, swung again, caught hold of another, swung once more, and landed with a thump that seemed to shake the sun-baked earth at the tree's foot. She shook herself once and came bounding over the grass.

She let herself through the wicket in the tall ironwork of the gates and came up to Miss Unwin.

"We'd better go for a walk if we want to talk secrets," she said. "If I stay in the grounds as I'm meant to, somebody's bound to come nosey-parkering."

"But won't you be missed? I don't like to—"

"Oh, pooh. If you never take risks, you never take fences. That's what Grandpapa says when he's off hunting, and so I don't jolly well see why I shouldn't take a risk or two myself."

Miss Unwin, the governess away in London, might have

had an answer to that. Miss Unwin, trying to save innocent Jack Steadman's life, kept her mouth shut.

When they were well out of sight of the lodge-keeper sitting out in the sun in her garden shelling peas, she wasted no time in asking Phemy what she wanted to know.

"Tell me about General Bickerstaffe," she said. "Tell me everything you've heard, no matter from whom."

"Oh, well," Phemy answered, "I know I oughtn't to discuss my elders and betters with the grooms and the gardeners and any others of the servants who aren't beastly starchy. But I can't help it when what they say's so interesting, can I? And now meeting you shows I was quite right all the time."

"If something you have learnt helps save Mr. Steadman," Miss Unwin answered, "you can feel that you've done right as long as you live."

"Well, then, old Billy Bickerstaffe. Let me see. First off, of course, he's had a quarrel with Grandpapa that began years and years ago, right after the war in the Crimea."

"Is that really true now? It doesn't seem to have prevented your grandfather inviting General Bickerstaffe to his ball."

"No, I'm not telling a bouncer, really. Grandpapa would never refuse old Billy an invitation. He couldn't. Not as a gentleman."

"Very well, I think I understand that. But what was this quarrel about?"

"Oh, only over what's the proper way of being a soldier. Grandpapa believes you shouldn't fight until you're made to, and old Billy always wanted to make the enemy do something that let him charge with his Heavy Brigade."

"I see."

Miss Unwin felt disappointed. Military theory was hardly going to provide anything that made General Bickerstaffe a victim for Alfie Goode's extortion.

"And then, oh, lots of other things," Phemy went blithely on. "I mean, old Billy was always having the troopers flogged and things like that, and Grandpapa always says they have a hard enough life anyway without being punished for the least thing."

Was there something there? Miss Unwin wondered. Had General Bickerstaffe once ordered Corporal Steadman to be flogged?

"Tell me," she said abruptly. "Your grandfather befriended Mr. Steadman. Do you remember what regiment he was in when he was a soldier?"

"Oh, yes. Grandpapa said such a lot about Mr. Steadman when they found him there in Hanger Wood like that. He wasn't a cavalry trooper at all, so Grandpapa was never his officer. He just got to know about him and that he had a splendid record. He was Ox and Bucks."

"Ox and Bucks?" asked Miss Unwin, who, however much she knew of history and geography, was no military expert.

"The Oxfordshire and Buckinghamshire Light Infantry. It's a jolly good regiment, Grandpapa says, even if it isn't cavalry."

"I see. And Bill—General Bickerstaffe, of course, was a cavalry officer, in the Heavy Brigade."

"Yes. And I think what really started the trouble between him and Grandpapa was that old Billy was furious all those years ago because the Light Brigade got all that glory in the Crimea. You know, having a poem written about them and everything. *When can their glory fade? O the wild charge they made!*"

"Yes," said Miss Unwin," I know. Into the Valley of Death."

"Oh, stars, yes. I never thought of that. You know what everybody round here, except the gentry, of course, calls where we're walking now?"

"Yes, indeed. The Valley of Death."

Phemy stopped their stroll. She looked suddenly pale.

"You don't think . . ." she said.

"No. Nonsense. Utter nonsense," Miss Unwin replied.

But she could not prevent herself remembering Mrs. De Lyall's two burly, stony-faced footmen up on the back of her carriage. Mrs. De Lyall had spoken only of rough treatment. But already one man had been killed to preserve the secret of the Valley of Death and another man was only hours away from dying, too. Was a similar fate awaiting her if she failed to leave the place by nightfall?

Then she saw that Phemy's face, which was not as clean as it might have been, was turning from pale to fiery red.

"No," she said to her firmly. "Any idea like that's just bosh, you know. Plain bosh. And now, what's my assistant detective got to tell me about General Bickerstaffe and Mrs. De Lyall?"

The appeal worked. Phemy's face resumed its normal healthy colour, and she set out along the lane once more.

"Well, he's spoony on her, of course," she said. "I think everybody round here knows that. Even Grandpapa. Even Mrs. Perker."

Miss Unwin hesitated before she put her next question. "And is . . . ?" And does . . . ?"

"If you mean, does he commit adultery with—"

"Oh, Phemy."

"Well, it's in the Bible, isn't it? So I suppose I'd be wicked, really, if I *didn't* know about it."

"Well, all right."

"A little bird tells me the answer actually is: Probably not."

"Little birds," Miss Unwin broke in sharply, the governess once more, "are generally more inventive than veracious."

Phemy looked at her curiously. But she was too keen to be the reliable detective's assistant to question this change.

"Well," she said, "really the bird was Fred, the stableboy. He told me when we were discussing it one day that you can never be certain sure with a thing like that, not unless you—"

"Phemy, that will do."

"Well, I thought a female detective wouldn't blush over just something like that."

"A female detective can be a lady, too."

"Oh, now you're the one talking bosh."

After which they walked along in silence. Miss Unwin was

thoughtful. A female detective could not, of course, be a lady. But on the other hand, if it was necessary in order to save the life of an innocent man to behave like a female detective, then that was what she was going to do. Lady or no lady.

"All right," she said at last, "tell me what your Fred thinks is the truth of the matter."

"Well," Phemy replied with a carelessness that Miss Unwin suspected was more than a little put on, "Fred thinks that, spoony though old Billy is, he hasn't actually committed you-know-what."

"I see. And you agree?"

"Yes. I mean, Billy's a bit like an old stallion, really. You just have to let them graze in the end, you know."

"I see," Miss Unwin said again.

For a little more they walked along in silence.

"Well," Miss Unwin resumed eventually, "I don't think there is anything more I need to know from you for the present. But I promise you, if there is, I shall come up to see you again as fast as I can."

"So have I really been a female detective's assistant?"

"Yes," said Miss Unwin, "I think you really have."

But walking back to the town, she found she had no more she could do to move things forward until the hour that evening when Arthur Burch would come driving down in his cart to sup his ale at the Rising Sun.

All she could do was to spend the afternoon in Mrs. Steadman's sitting-room, reading over and over again the details of the trial pasted in the old account-book. She had hoped that somehow she would, after all, manage to hit on something that Mr. Serjeant Busfield had not noticed when he had been conducting Jack Steadman's defence. But it was an ill-founded hope, as she had really feared all along that it would be.

So it was a decided relief when at about five o'clock the maidservant, Betsey, knocked on the door bearing a tea-tray. Though she did not think she had any appetite even for a piece of Mrs. Steadman's fruit-cake, a cup of tea would be more than welcome.

"Betsey," she said as the girl carefully lowered the tray, "have you seen your mistress this afternoon? How is she? Can you tell me?"

The tea-tray dropped the last inch onto the table with a sharp crash. A deep red flush sprang up on the white column of the girl's neck.

"Oh, miss, miss," she blurted out. "The mistress is bad, very bad. How can you think anything else when—when the master's to be hanged come Friday?"

And, without waiting for any comment Miss Unwin might have, she blundered round and ran out the door.

Rising to close it after her, Miss Unwin was decidedly thoughtful.

But almost at once the recollection of what was to happen down below in the private bar in not much more than an hour put everything else out of her head.

She longed to hear from Mr. Heavitree. Perhaps, after all, he had seen his quarry make a dash for freedom and had caught him. And then . . . ? Had Arthur Burch already given him the name of the man who had persuaded him to give his false evidence?

She wished now that, instead of sitting uselessly going over the reports of the trial, she had trudged through the hot sunshine out to the farmer's isolated cottage once again and had somehow found Mr. Heavitree in his watcher's hiding-place.

But she knew this was nonsense. If her fellow detective was secretly watching the farmer, he would not be easily found, and she herself making her way along the lane, which she knew could be seen from either of the two upper windows of the cottage, would be quite likely to have been spotted. And that would mean Arthur Burch would know that her interest in him was more than that of a lady magazine writer who had been easily scared away by the sight of his shotgun. So the long-waited-for effect of a shock revelation would be wasted.

No, she must continue to be patient until the farmer was well established in the bar down below. Then she and Mr. Heavitree could make their entrance side by side, and that, if they had judged their man correctly, would cause his nerve to break.

Yet it would be a relief to hear Mr. Heavitree's solid tread on the stairs just now, and to be able to discuss with him the final details of the ruse.

But no sound came.

Down below, all was bustle as the inn prepared for its business of the evening. Briefly Miss Unwin wondered how Mrs. Steadman was managing without the assistance of Vilkins, washing glasses and running errands. And Betsey? With that odd behaviour of hers, those sudden, deep, not easily explained blushes at the mention, surely, of her master's predicament, would she be as helpful behind the bar as she ought to be?

Time passed. From the window of the sitting-room Miss Unwin, kneeling on the sofa to peer out as far as she could, was able to observe customers coming for their evening's entertainment. There were plenty of them. And no wonder, she thought. It is not every day in a man's life when he can drink his ale in a house where the landlord is to be hanged before the week is out.

There were plenty of customers. But there was no sign of Mr. Heavitree. What had happened to him? Had he set out in chase of Arthur Burch and had the farmer perhaps turned that gun of his on him?

She left the window and began to pace round and round the little room.

Surely if Arthur Burch had made a break for it and had been held and had confessed, Mr. Heavitree would have hastened back to the Rising Sun with the news. Mrs. Steadman had a right to know as soon as it was humanly possible, even if Miss Unwin might be supposed to be able to possess her soul in patience.

She went back to the sofa and craned again out the open window into the soft evening air.

And then she saw a cart drawn by a scraggy horse coming meandering along towards the inn. She knew at once, even before she had got a clear sight of the man loosely holding the reins of an animal well acquainted with the way, who it would be.

Arthur Burch. Arthur Burch coming to take his evening's refreshment below. The cautious beast coming all unwarily to the set trap.

But where was Mr. Heavitree?

12

Watching Arthur Burch arrive at the Rising Sun, Miss Unwin saw his horse appear to come to a halt without any check from its master, slumped on the seat of his battered old cart. For two or three minutes he stayed where he was, looking dully at the road in front of him. Then at last he heaved himself up and jumped clumsily to the ground.

Drunk, Miss Unwin realised. Arthur Burch was more than a little drunk even before coming to the inn.

She welcomed the discovery. It showed he was already a deeply worried man. No doubt he had not been entirely happy about the danger of being found to have given perjured evidence at Jack Steadman's trial. He must have known that what he had said in the witness-box was what had sealed that verdict of guilty. And now, within days of the morning when Jack Steadman was to hang, to have people come asking him about that evidence must have added suddenly to his fears. Even the sluggish conscience that had enabled him night after night to visit the very home of the man he was sending to death must have surely been touched.

Was he already, forgetting altogether to tie his horse to one of the posts outside the inn as he staggered inside, at the point where he would break?

Oh, where, where was Mr. Heavitree?

Miss Unwin leant even farther out the window and strained to see along the road. But there was not the least sign of the former detective.

Abruptly, she decided that what she ought to do if she could was to keep Arthur Burch under observation herself.

What if some chance remark from another customer in the private bar did what she and Mr. Heavitree had planned to do by confronting the perjurer out of the blue themselves? What if he poured out some sort of confession to ears that did not know enough to appreciate its full meaning?

She hurried downstairs.

But in the passage dividing the two bars she came to a halt. She realised she was in more than a little of a difficulty. Arthur Burch might well be sitting staring directly out the open doorway of the private bar, and only by standing in or near that doorway could she keep watch on him. It was where he had been sitting when, according to his evidence at the assizes, he had heard the exact words Alfie Goode had flung from the doorway of the taproom opposite at Jack Steadman behind him.

She decided she must risk at least taking one quick look.

Gathering herself up, she launched into a rapid walk that would take her straight past the open doorway. As she passed, she would turn her head quickly and trust that she would spot Arthur Burch before he, in his state of drunken bemusement, noticed her.

One, two, three, four quick steps. Turn the head. And yes. Yes, there he was, slumped on a settle in the far corner. Mercifully, his head was so sunk on his breast that he could not have seen her.

Out in the road where the setting sun was casting long purplish shadows, she stopped and thought. In a moment she realised she had seen more than she had thought. Besides the half-drunk farmer slouched on the settle, she had seen the small window almost directly over his head.

Through that, if she could get up to it from outside, she would surely be able to keep him under observation, completely safe herself.

She hurried round to the side of the inn. The narrow path leading to the back of the building was deserted and already dusky. She looked for the window. Yes, there it was, high up and partly obscured by ivy growing up the side wall.

But was it too high to reach? And below it nettles grew in a formidable clump.

She looked round. Nothing to stand on. Quietly she walked on round the corner to the inn's backyard. There was no one about.

But, almost as if it had been put there by the sheer power of wishing, she saw at once the wooden wash-tub which that morning Vilkins had had her arms in up to the elbows in soapy suds. She had left it propped against the back wall to drain.

Miss Unwin looked about cautiously and approached the tub. It was heavy indeed to lift, but deep as it was it would surely make a stand high enough for her to be able to peer through that tiny window.

She grasped it with both arms as if it was a great fat man she was about to dance with. She bent at the knees and heaved. The tub came up with her.

At an ungainly staggering walk, she got it round to the path beside the inn and at last, plonk, let it drop into the middle of the clump of nettles.

It was the work of a moment then to lift her skirts and, clutching at a thick ivy stem on the wall, to hoist herself up onto the upturned tub. She found that her face was bang in front of the window.

In the private bar a lamp had just been lit, and by the light it cast it was easy to see the top of Arthur Burch's battered and dirty hat directly underneath her. And there was something else to see, too.

On the narrow, rough wooden table in front of the farmer there was not the pot of ale that had been his customary tipple. Instead there was a glass with in it, she could see quite distinctly, the bright brown glint of brandy and soda. Arthur Burch was evidently determined to blot out any pangs of conscience and the fear of discovery.

But how much more drunk was he going to get?

At the moment he appeared to be content to sit solitary and brood over his troubles. But drink could go any way. It might need only another sip of that brandy to make him lurch off to anyone who would listen and pour out all his woes.

And she would not be there to hear if he let out a name, the name of the man who had paid or persuaded him to give his false evidence. The name of the man who had shot Alfie Goode in the back of the head and then had arranged for Jack Steadman to be suspected and tried for the crime.

Where was Mr. Heavitree? Surely, the right moment to play their trick had now come?

But there was nothing she could do except stay where she was and hope that no one came along the path between the inn and the next-door cottage. Dusk, thank goodness, was creeping on, and at least she would not be easily seen by any passers-by in the road.

She stood and watched.

Arthur Burch finished his glass and called for another. Betsey, who was behind the bar, brought it over to him and said something as she took his money. It was impossible to hear what it was, thanks to the murmur of talk in the room, but from the sharp expression on the girl's face Miss Unwin guessed she had been telling the farmer that he had had almost all the drink she was prepared to let him have.

The path at her back was now quite dark, although above the sky still held light.

Patiently, she turned back to the window and the sight of Arthur Burch's dirty old hat and the twinkling glass of brandy on the table in front of him. He was putting the glass to his lips only at long intervals, as if he had taken some heed of Betsey's warning. But each time he reached out, his hand seemed to waver more, and it was plain that he was now very, very drunk.

Then suddenly there came from the entrance to the path some five or six yards away a tiny scuffling sound.

And, Miss Unwin remembered with an abrupt chill, it was nightfall.

With her mind fixed on Arthur Burch, she had not thought at all about Mrs. De Lyall's threat. It had been something she had made up her mind to ignore, and she had now forgotten it altogether. But what if, while she had been wholly engrossed in keeping watch on the farmer, Mrs. De Lyall's bully boys had been on the look-out for her? They could have been lurking on the other side of the road already when she had come hurrying out, and then they might have waited watching her until night had fully fallen, the last limit Mrs. De Lyall had allowed her.

There came another sound from the entrance to the path, a distinct footfall.

Miss Unwin, her face pressed against the little window, did not dare to turn.

Another stealthy footfall.

Could she jump from her perch, dash into the backyard of the inn, and find somewhere to hide? In a shed or somewhere? Or batter on the back door and shout for all she was worth?

"Miss Unwin. It's you. I wondered."

The familiar solid voice of Mr. Heavitree.

Miss Unwin felt such a surge of relief that she almost fell from the tub.

"Miss Unwin? Are you all right? You look disturbed."

She turned. Mr. Heavitree was standing right behind her.

"Yes. Yes, Mr. Heavitree. It was just that— But never mind. You're here now, and Arthur Burch is sitting in the taproom just underneath this window. Very drunk."

"Yes, I looked in at the front door and saw him. I'm sorry I couldn't get here earlier, but he left home in his cart sooner than I expected, and I've had to foot it all the way back."

It is always the simple explanation, Miss Unwin thought.

"Well, no matter," she said. "Don't you think, though, it is time we played our trick?"

"Yes, my dear, I do. If he's only half as drunk as you've said, he'll be more than ripe for it."

Mr. Heavitree held out a hand to her. She took it and jumped from the tub.

"Then let's try," she said.

What they decided they had to do was very simple. They merely walked in at the front entrance of the inn and placed themselves at the door of the private bar. Arthur Burch was sitting there still, swaying backwards and forwards over the last remains of his brandy.

"If he stays like that, he won't even see us," Miss Unwin said.

"Oh, he'll look up sooner or later," Mr. Heavitree replied. "And if he doesn't, I'll rouse him soon enough."

They stood in the doorway for another minute or two. But for all the notice the drunken farmer took of them, they might have been in Timbuktu.

"All right," Mr. Heavitree said at last, "I'll try this." He took a pace backwards so that he was standing facing well into the room. "Yes," he said in a voice so loud it even startled Miss Unwin, "Arthur Burch could never have heard those words from where he's sitting."

It was enough, and more than enough.

At the sound of his name echoing out, the farmer looked up bemusedly. And there, clear in his line of vision, was Miss Unwin plainly engaged in conversation with the police officer who had wanted to know about the evidence he had given at Jack Steadman's trial.

He sat staring at the pair of them with his face moment by moment draining of all colour.

It's as white as a sheet of letter-paper, Miss Unwin thought. It really is.

Then the victim of their device lurched to his feet. He sent the narrow table in front of him crashing over with a thud, stepped over it in a single stride, and came straight towards them.

And, Miss Unwin realised, drunk though he had been till a minute before, he was now stone-cold sober.

At the doorway, which Mr. Heavitree continued to block, he came to a halt.

"You devils," he said. "You utter devils."

His face under the thick thatch of dark hair was filled with cold anger.

Will he say more? Miss Unwin asked herself. Is he going to break now, as we calculated?

But the shock they had administered seemed to have done its work too well. It had indeed sobered the drunken farmer, put him in mind of just what he had done and what he could be made to suffer because of it.

"Get out of my way," he snarled at Mr. Heavitree. "Get out of my way, now and for ever."

Mr. Heavitree stepped aside. Arthur Burch gave him a single glare of bitter hatred and then, pushing past Miss Unwin in a wave of brandy-soaked breath, he marched out into the road.

"You let him go?" Miss Unwin said.

"Oh, yes, I let him go," Mr. Heavitree answered. "It hasn't worked, you see. He won't talk now. But in time he will. Tomorrow, when the brandy fire's gone out."

"Yes. Yes, I suppose so. But—but, Mr. Heavitree, what about tonight? When he gets home and begins to think? Won't he . . . ? Mightn't he . . . ? Mr. Heavitree, he has a shotgun, you know."

The old detective looked grim. "Yes," he said slowly. "Yes, damn it, he might."

Without a moment's thought, Miss Unwin wheeled round and ran out of the house into the road.

She saw that Arthur Burch had found his horse peacefully tugging at a clump of grass not far from the post he had failed to tie it to when he had arrived. He had clambered up onto the cart and now, with no more than a muttered oath, started his obedient animal off on its way back to his distant cottage.

Miss Unwin did not hesitate. She ran. She ran as hard as she could go and in a few strides caught up the slowly moving cart. Again she did not hesitate. She seized the backboard and heaved herself up. Her scrabbling legs found somewhere to put themselves. She looked ahead. Seated like a lifeless sack on the seat in front, Arthur Burch had taken no notice whatsoever of the swing and sway of the cart as she had got onto it.

For a minute and then another, she clung where she was. The horse plodded forward through the soft summer darkness. Arthur Burch sat slumped behind it.

Miss Unwin hauled herself farther up. She could see right into the cart now. It was a quarter full of hay, hay that a better farmer would long ago have cleared out from it.

Cautiously, never taking her eyes off the slouching figure in front, careless of her skirts, Miss Unwin got first one leg and then the other over the backboard. She crouched low. Still the farmer was oblivious of her presence. She slid down till she was lying full-length at the back of the old cart. With care, she began gathering the hay in it towards her. It smelt abominable. She paid no attention. In some five minutes she had more or less covered herself with the wretched, half-rotten stuff.

Then she lay still as the cart slowly jogged its way along towards the isolated cottage.

If when Arthur Burch arrived there his conscience had emerged enough from the alcoholic fumes that had once more doused it, she intended to be there, close to him, ready to wrest his gun from his hands if that was the way his thoughts took him. And then she would make him confess.

13

Farmer Burch's old horse jogged on through the summer night. Miss Unwin lay on her back on the floor of the cart, the acid-smelling hay over her in a prickly layer.

Arthur Burch himself seemed locked again in the state of heavy drunkenness he had been in before Mr. Heavitree had given him the fright which, unfortunately for their plans, had shocked him into soberness. He swayed from side to side up on the seat, and from time to time Miss Unwin caught muttered words.

"Lady writer. Lady writer. I knew she . . . Should have put some shot into . . . Ha, ha. That would've . . . Damned policeman, why couldn't . . . ? Should be in his grave. In his grave, in his grave. Peace. Got to have . . . Like to've seen her full of shot. Ha! Ha, ha."

But carefully though Miss Unwin listened to these ramblings, Arthur Burch never once referred in any way to what it was that had caused them: the perjured evidence he had given at the assizes.

No doubt, he was still gripped by a fierce intention never to admit to his crime, and this was preventing him even in his state of drunkenness from speaking aloud as much as a single word that might give away his secret.

At last the horse turned at the great oak spreading over the whole road at the start of the lane leading to the farm. Miss Unwin, cautiously raising her head from its covering of black hay, saw the cottage starkly silhouetted against the starlit sky. She continued to lie where she was. It did not seem likely that the drunken farmer would look into the back of the cart when they arrived. She calculated that, if she wanted to make sure he did not use his shotgun on himself, she could do no better than stay still until he had left the cart.

But what she had failed to take into account was what would happen when he took the horse out of the shafts. This, after much cursing and swearing in the darkness, he eventually managed to do.

With a sudden crashing swing, the cart upended itself. Lying near its back, Miss Unwin was not hurled very far by the upheaval, but, banged hard against the backboard, she had to clench her teeth grimly to prevent herself crying out.

Lying in an undignified heap at the bottom of the upended cart, she heard Arthur Burch give his freed horse a slap that sent it trotting softly off into the field beside the garden. Then, muttering incoherently, the farmer made his way towards the house.

Miss Unwin rose from her sprawled position. Her left knee was shooting with pain, and the whole of her left side felt battered. But she managed to get to her feet and extricate herself from the cart without making too much noise.

She drew in a deep breath and peered into the darkness. She thought she could make out that Arthur Burch had pushed open the door of the cottage. No doubt, it was left unlocked in this remote part—and with, she remembered, his old mother in occupation.

Then she heard distinctly the sound of a match being struck. A light sprang up where she had thought the open door was. She crept forward.

In the passageway of the cottage she saw the farmer putting, with wavering hand, the match-flame to a candle standing on a bench just inside the door.

What would he do next? Would he stagger off to bed? Or would he make his way into the kitchen? And if he did, would he see the shotgun in the corner where he had seized it to threaten her? And then . . . ? Then would he attempt to take his own life? And would she be able to rush in, snatch the weapon from him, and force him afterwards to say who it was who had persuaded him to give his false testimony?

Getting hold of the gun, she thought, should be within her powers. If she acted with resolution. Arthur Burch was so drunk that he would scarcely be able to resist, or be quick enough to swing the gun round to confront her once more.

She advanced boldly across the tussocky grass in front of the cottage.

She was within three yards of the door when, with another oath, Arthur Burch kicked it shut.

Miss Unwin stepped quickly back so as to get a good view of the whole of the cottage and its windows. Would the light show itself in the kitchen on the right, or the bedroom she had glimpsed on her earlier visit on the left?

She waited.

In the darkness a big night-beetle went droning by.

And the light, somewhat to her surprise, appeared in one of the two windows of the cottage's upper storey. So apparently that better-kept bedroom she had seen did not belong to the tenant.

Well, she thought, at least he has not gone to the kitchen. So I shall not, I trust, have to wrest that gun from him. And, alas, I shall not be able to force a confession from him now.

She stayed where she was in the neglected patch of garden, staring up at the light in the window. Before long she actually saw Arthur Burch outlined against it. He tossed away somewhere the old hat he had managed to keep on his head. Then he took off his jacket and evidently allowed it to slip down onto the floor. Next he moved away from the window, and at last the candle was extinguished.

Miss Unwin remained on the watch for almost half an hour more, occasionally looking up at the window. But there was no sign of activity behind its dark panes. For the rest of the time, she busied herself in brushing from her dress any still-clinging pieces of rotten hay. But at last she felt it safe to set off again on the weary walk back to Chipping Compton.

Limping along, she met Mr. Heavitree about half-way, and felt grateful at once that, tired as he must be, he had plodded off in search of her.

"All's well," she called as soon as she recognised in the light of the newly risen moon the familiar figure. "He's safely in bed, and I dare say with all that drink in him he'll be there well into tomorrow morning."

"Good," said Mr. Heavitree. "A fine piece of work, my dear. I'm too old and too portly to go chasing after a cart the way you did. But it's the better for being done. And tomorrow you and I will present ourselves again at Master Burch's. If he feels half as ill as I think he will, he won't be in a state to resist a few sharp questions then."

With this comforting thought, Miss Unwin managed to get herself back to the Rising Sun in good spirits. She tumbled into bed filled with a determination to be up early next day.

But she did not wake, in fact, until there came a vigorous tapping on her door.

"Come in," she called.

It was Betsey.

"Sorry to wake you so early, miss," she said. "Only, the gentleman was so earnest."

"What gentleman?" Miss Unwin said, groping for her watch, which she had laid on the floor beside the bed.

She saw that it was just after six.

"I think his name be Mr. Heavitree, miss," Betsey answered.

"And he wants me to come down to him?"

"That he do."

A sudden terrible thought came to Miss Unwin.

"He was in earnest, you say? Was he very urgent? Did he say that—that something had happened?"

"Oh, no, miss. It was just that he said you wouldn't mind being wakened, though it was late when you got to bed."

"Very well," Miss Unwin answered, relieved. "Would you tell him I shall be down in ten minutes?"

"That I will."

Betsey turned to the door. But at it she paused and looked back at Miss Unwin, who had begun to throw back the bedcovers.

"Oh, miss," she said.

Miss Unwin looked at her sharply. "Yes? Yes, what is it?"

"No, nothing, miss. You'll be wanting to get down to see Mr. Heavitree."

"I am. But if you have anything of importance you want to say to me . . ."

"No. No, miss. It ain't so important. Not truly."

"Very well, then."

Betsey closed the door, leaving Miss Unwin thoughtful. But she had no time now to consider what in all probability was only a young girl's fancy of some sort. Hastily she went to the washstand, poured cold water into its basin, and washed.

She was down to see Mr. Heavitree in just less than her ten minutes.

"Mr. Heavitree, there's nothing . . . ?"

"No, my dear. But I got to thinking as I went back to my sister's last night after seeing you to here that if perchance our friend should wake early, he might—you know."

"Yes, he might."

"So I've come with a little trap I've borrowed, and we can be at the cottage in ten minutes."

"I'm glad," Miss Unwin said.

The trap, with a neat, fresh-looking horse in its shafts, was waiting outside. She climbed in and took her seat next to Mr. Heavitree. He touched the horse with the end of his whip and they were off at a sharp trot.

But, as they went up the lane leading to the cottage, they saw that they were not the first people to call there that day.

Standing in the garden, looking up into the blue morning sky, was a police constable and outside there was a smart wagonette, its horse tethered to one of the posts of the sagging wooden gate.

Mr. Heavitree whipped up their own animal and, as soon as they were within calling distance, shouted out to the constable.

"It's Grigson, isn't it? You remember me? Mr. Heavitree, late of the Metropolitan. What's happening here?"

"It's Farmer Burch, Mr. Heavitree," the constable answered. "Shot himself, he has. Nasty business."

Miss Unwin and Mr. Heavitree looked at one another.

Slowly, Mr. Heavitree got down from the trap and tied the horse's reins to the other post of the broken-down gate.

"When did this happen?" he asked.

"Lord knows just when, Mr. Heavitree. Dr. Podgers is looking at the body now. He came with Inspector Whatmough."

"Did he? And how did you get to know about this, so early in the day?"

"Ah, that was young Tom Featherby. Helps at the farm here, when Arthur Burch thinks o' something for him to do."

"I see. Well, I'll go in. I may have something to tell Mr. Whatmough."

"I s'pose that'll be all right," the constable said doubtfully.

Mr. Heavitree gave him no time for second thoughts.

Neither did Miss Unwin.

She had got down from the trap while Mr. Heavitree had been asking his questions and had gone unobtrusively up the weed-strewn path to the cottage door. Now she simply followed Mr. Heavitree in.

The first thing she saw, or rather heard, was an old woman sitting on the bottom stair at the far end of the entrance passage moaning to herself in quiet desperation.

Arthur Burch's mother, of course, she thought.

She went forward to give her what comfort she could.

But, as she did so, she could not help taking one long

careful glance into the kitchen where, she knew, that shotgun had rested in a corner.

She saw that Arthur Burch was lying on his back in the middle of the floor with his head an appalling mess of blood. In his right hand there still lay the gun, which evidently he had put to his face before pulling the trigger.

The doctor was kneeling beside the body, and behind him there stood Inspector Whatmough, smart in his uniform.

Miss Unwin, thrusting the sight of the body firmly from her mind, went up to the dead man's mother.

"Mrs. Burch?"

The old woman made no attempt to answer or even look up. Her insistent moaning went on as before.

"Mrs. Burch, this must have been terrible for you," Miss Unwin said. "Terrible."

Still the quiet moaning went on.

Miss Unwin slid down to sit on the stair beside the old woman. She put her arm round her shoulders.

"Look," she said, "let me take you somewhere where you'll be more comfortable."

She got no response.

"Let me take you into the bedroom there," she said, indicating the other room on the ground floor. "You'll be better lying down."

But now the old woman did break off for a moment in her keening grief.

"No," she said in a sudden shout. "Not there. Not allowed. No."

Miss Unwin did not attempt to find out why Arthur Burch's mother apparently was not permitted in that room.

"Well, let me help you upstairs," she said again. "You will be better lying down. Really, you will. And I will try to make you some tea."

Gently, she attempted to raise the old woman. Her body, light as a bird's, came up in Miss Unwin's grasp. Almost carrying her, she got up the stairs step by step. At the top she remembered the outline of the now-dead farmer she had seen the night before against the wavering candlelight and steered her burden into the room on the other side. She picked the old woman up bodily and put her on the low, unmade bed.

Not for a moment since her outburst at the suggestion of going into the downstairs bedroom had the old woman ceased her moaning, quiet and nerve-grating.

Miss Unwin looked down at her with compassion.

"Now I will see if I can make tea," she said.

The old woman made no reply, directly. But she did raise herself a little on the bed.

"No," she moaned. "No, no, no."

"You don't want tea? It will do you good."

"Stay."

It had been hard to make out what the word was, but Miss Unwin thought she had been begged not to go.

"Of course I'll stay," she said. "I'll stay as long as you want. But I could go and make some tea and be back in a few minutes. You ought to take something. You've had no breakfast. I noticed the table laid for it as I went past."

"Shutter," the old woman said, pronouncing the word with sudden blurred force. "Shutter. Shutter."

"The light is hurting your eyes? I'll close the shutters certainly."

Miss Unwin moved over to the single square window.

"Oh, but there are no shutters," she said. "And no curtains either, I'm afraid."

"Shutter. Shutter." Miss Unwin looked round the small room in desperation. At last she saw a tattered red cloth on the chest of drawers.

"Look," she said, "perhaps I can put this up against the window, if the light really does hurt you."

"Shutter, shutter, shutter."

"Yes, yes. I'm doing the best I can."

With difficulty Miss Unwin pushed open the casement,

draped the red cloth over its two halves, and banged them sharply back into place. Her rough effort appeared to have done the trick. The shabby cloth was blotting out most of the light.

"There," she said, "is that better?"

But the old woman had turned her face away and had begun to moan again, though more quietly than before.

"I'll fetch some tea," Miss Unwin said.

She went down to the kitchen. Either the doctor or the inspector had found a tablecloth and spread it over Arthur Burch's body. Together with Mr. Heavitree, they were standing near it, talking gravely.

"I think I ought to tell you," Mr. Heavitree was saying, "it's my belief he had good reason."

Miss Unwin had not intended to do more than see if the fire was alight in the kitchen range and find a kettle to make tea. But at Mr. Heavitree's words she turned to the solemn little group.

"You're suggesting Mr. Burch killed himself?" she said.

Inspector Whatmough frowned at her. "I don't know who you are, young woman," he said. "But it is at least clear that that is precisely what has happened."

"No," said Miss Unwin. "It is not what has happened. Arthur Burch has been murdered."

14

All three of the men standing near the sprawled body of Arthur Burch turned towards Miss Unwin. Dr. Podgers, his tall hat in his hand with his stethoscope returned to its customary place inside it, looked merely puzzled. Inspector Whatmough, thin and grizzled, looked fiercely angry. Even Mr. Heavitree, the most experienced in murder of the three and Miss Unwin's champion, wore an expression of sad disappointment.

But before Miss Unwin could offer any explanation of her claim that, despite the shotgun loosely held in Farmer Burch's hand, he had not killed himself, the sound of a horse's galloping hooves was heard from outside.

Inspector Whatmough went across to the low window, stooped, and peered out.

"Yes," he said, "I thought as much. It's my Chief Constable."

Major Charteris, Miss Unwin thought. Major Charteris, the Tartar.

The galloping hooves came to a halt. "Here, you, catch the reins," they heard the Major shout to Constable Grigson in the garden. Then the man himself was standing at the kitchen door.

Miss Unwin saw that he was a decidedly formidable figure. Though perhaps in his late fifties, he still retained all the fiercely upright carriage of the soldier. This air of military aggressiveness was reinforced by a mottled, outdoor complexion and a strong, if greying, pair of moustaches like the horns of a head-lowered bull.

"Right," he snapped, his voice echoing into the low-ceilinged room with parade-ground force, "what is all this I hear, Whatmough? Burch committed suicide? Always thought the fellow was peculiar. My tenant, you know. Came to me with the estate."

Inspector Whatmough drew himself up to attention. "Yes, sir," he said. "Suicide. A clear case, thank goodness. His own shotgun, still in his hand."

"Good. Good. Thought I'd better look in. Death occurring on my own land and all that. But you'll deal with everything, Whatmough. Make sure the coroner has all the particulars exactly. No damned slipshod work, d'you hear?"

"Yes, sir. You can rely on me."

Major Charteris, slapping his booted leg with the riding whip he carried, turned to go.

"One moment, if you please," said Miss Unwin.

Major Charteris wheeled round. "You spoke to me, madam? I am not at all clear just what you are doing here? Death chamber and all that."

"I am here because I had some questions I wished to put to Mr. Burch," Miss Unwin said, loudly and clearly. "But I find he was murdered before I had a chance to speak to him."

"Murdered?" Major Charteris exploded.

"I was about to tell the young woman that she was talking nonsense, sir," Inspector Whatmough put in hastily.

"Quite right."

Again the Chief Constable turned to go.

But now Mr. Heavitree spoke up.

"Excuse me, sir," he said. "Perhaps you'll remember me. Heavitree, former Superintendent at Scotland Yard."

Major Charteris gave him a quick look. It did not appear to acknowledge their acquaintanceship as being very valuable to him.

"I think, sir," Mr. Heavitree said, undeterred, "that it might be worth your while at least to listen to what Miss

Unwin here has to say. She's a remarkably intelligent person, sir, you may take my word for it."

"Intelligent? I dare say. But she is a woman, damn it."

"Yes, sir," Mr. Heavitree said. "And I will admit I don't see myself why this death is anything other than what it appears to be. But nevertheless I would respectfully advise you, sir, to hear Miss Unwin out."

"You would, would you? All right, then, madam. You have two minutes."

Miss Unwin drew herself up. "I shall not need two minutes," she said. "All I would ask you to do is to direct your attention to the table here."

The Chief Constable shot a glance from under formidable eyebrows at the simple kitchen table.

"Well? A perfectly ordinary table, for a cottage. None too clean, I see, but Burch always was . . . Still, mustn't speak ill of the dead, I suppose."

"A perfectly ordinary table, yes," said Miss Unwin. "Laid for breakfast last night in quite the ordinary way. There is the teapot in front of old Mrs. Burch's place, and there opposite her is her son's place. With the knife on its left-hand side."

"And what of that?" Major Charteris barked.

But Mr. Heavitree was ahead of him.

"Knife on the left, sir," he said. "A left-handed man. But that gun is in the fellow's right hand. Miss Unwin's correct, sir. She's correct, after all. This is murder. Murder disguised as suicide."

The Chief Constable stood there silent. His mouth under his ferocious moustache was turned grimly down.

At last he turned to Inspector Whatmough. "Well, Inspector?"

The Inspector sighed. "I think there may be something in what Mr. Heavitree says, sir," he replied.

"Something in what Miss Unwin has said," Mr. Heavitree corrected him.

"Yes, I dare say," Major Charteris grunted. "I dare say."

Again he turned to Inspector Whatmough. "Well, man, if you've got a murder inquiry on your hands, you'd better not be standing there gawping. Get on with it, get on with it. I shall be back home for luncheon. Come over then and have something to report."

He swung away and marched out. They heard him bark something at Constable Grigson and then the brisk clop of hooves.

Inspector Whatmough turned to Mr. Heavitree. "Something to report," he said bitterly. "By one o'clock, if you please. Why, since that man came here it's been nothing but shouted orders and parades and marching. He may be the hero of the Alma and all that, but I can't see Army ways being much help with police work."

Then he, too, strode out and could be heard a moment later taking the unfortunate Grigson to task.

Mr. Heavitree looked at Miss Unwin. "Well," he said, "we were too late, were we not? Whoever it was that killed Alfie Goode, and persuaded poor Burch to tell his lies in court, got here before us."

Miss Unwin sighed. "Yes, that's true enough. But it does tell us one thing."

"That we're on the right road?"

"No," Miss Unwin said, "something more than that. It tells us that whoever we're looking for is very much in this particular part of the world. He's been able to keep a close watch over whatever we've been doing."

"Yes. Yes, you're right. And I must say I don't much like it."

"But I do like it," Miss Unwin retorted. "The nearer he is to us, that man, the nearer we are to him. And we have only tomorrow left in which to lay him by the heels."

"Yes, I take your point, my dear. And I'll tell you one piece of good news in exchange."

"Good news? After this?" Miss Unwin looked across to the body hidden under the tablecloth.

"Well, better news than it might be. The Chief Constable,

when we go to him with a name—if ever we get that name—
he won't be half as difficult to handle now after what you've
just demonstrated to him."

"Well," Miss Unwin answered, "we must hope not. But,
good gracious, I'm forgetting all about that poor woman upstairs. I came down to make her some tea."

She turned and bustled about, looking for kettle and tea-
caddy.

It did not take her long to make the tea, and she hurried
upstairs with a cup. Mrs. Burch was lying in almost the same
position as she had left her on the unmade bed. But, though
she still gave out a groan from time to time, the continuous
moaning had ceased.

"Let me help you to sit," Miss Unwin said.

She heaved the frail old woman higher in the bed and
offered her the tea. Tremblingly she took the cup, but in
trying to lift it to her lips she began spilling it.

Miss Unwin took the cup from her.

"I had better mop that mess up," she said.

She peered at Mrs. Burch, trying to see in the half darkness
in which the red cloth over the window had left the room
how much tea had been spilt.

"Would you mind now if I gave us a little more light?" she
asked.

The old woman looked over at the window.

"What did you put that there for?" she demanded with
sudden querulousness. "My best cloth."

Miss Unwin privately thought that if the tattered cloth she
had taken from the top of the chest of drawers was Mrs.
Burch's best, her others must be little more than rags. But she
kept silent.

She went over to the window, carefully removed her im-
provised curtain, and restored it to its place.

"I thought you had asked me to close the shutters," she
said, by way of keeping Mrs. Burch's thought away from her
loss.

The old woman gave a shrieking gasp.

Miss Unwin turned and hurried across to the bed.

"What is it? Whatever is it?"

Frightened eyes stared up at her.

"Please, Mrs. Burch, you're in trouble. Tell me what it is. Perhaps I can help."

"He'll come," the old woman whispered. "He'll come."

"Who will come, Mrs. Burch? You can tell me."

"He killed my Arthur. He'll kill me, too."

Miss Unwin's pulses raced. Was she going to hear after all from this trembling old woman the name Arthur Burch had been killed to prevent her learning?

"Yes, Mrs. Burch, yes?" she said. "Tell me who it was. Then the police can come and arrest him, and you'll be safe."

"Police? No, no."

"Yes, Mrs. Burch. Yes. Perhaps your son did something the police would not approve of, but they approve of murder much less. Tell me who it was who killed him. Just tell me, and soon all this will be over."

The old woman looked up at her with blinking, frightened eyes. Miss Unwin smelt suddenly the sour odour of the bed-clothes under her.

"Mrs. Burch," she said, "you must tell me that name. Justice demands it."

"Justice?"

"Yes. The man who murdered your son, he can be brought to justice. Who was it, Mrs. Burch?"

Again silence and the blinking of scared old eyes. And then a whisper. Faint as a dying puff of breeze.

"Sutter."

For a moment Miss Unwin thought the half-crazed old woman had reverted to her mania about the light and was wanting the nonexistent shutters on the window closed again. But then a different thought came to her. Perhaps the old woman had not been as incoherent as she had assumed. Perhaps she had really meant to say "Sutter."

"His name was Sutter? A man called Sutter killed your son?"

"Mr. Sutter. Mr. Sutter."

"And you know this? You know that it was him?"

There had been no name of Sutter on the list of guests at General Pastell's ball, Miss Unwin was sure of that. Yet she supposed that it was possible there had been some gentleman in the district who had not been invited, despite what Mrs. Perker had said. There might be some recluse living nearby. Or someone who was not quite a gentleman.

She felt the blood course through her veins. She was within moments of finding her quarry now. Within moments. And within hours perhaps Jack Steadman would be safe.

But the old woman was murmuring again.

"He came. Last night. Very late. He came. I heard a noise. . . ."

"Yes? You heard a noise? You went downstairs? You saw Mr. Sutter shoot your son?"

"No, no, no."

Miss Unwin's heart plummeted. "But I thought you said . . ."

"Arthur told me . . . keep out o' the way. When he came. Whenever he came."

"Mr. Sutter? He came here regularly?"

"That woman. Arthur said . . . mind own business. But last night it was so late, and voices . . . Angry . . ."

"You heard voices raised in anger last night and you went downstairs?"

"Then a shot, and . . . and . . ."

"And you crept back up here? Of course you did. It was the best thing to do. But did you see Mr. Sutter last night?"

"Voice," the old woman murmured.

"Ah, you heard his voice? You recognised it? Are you sure?"

"I know it. Well. Well."

"Yes. Good. And now tell me, who is Mr. Sutter? Where does he live?"

"Don't know."

"But—but you must."

Miss Unwin strove to suppress the anger she felt. How could this old woman, this vital witness, not know anything more than the bare name of the man she was certain had murdered her son?

She took a deep breath. "Mrs. Burch," she said, "tell me what Mr. Sutter looks like, if you really don't know where he comes from."

"Never proper sight of him. But I know that voice. Know that any time."

Miss Unwin thought. "It was a gentleman's voice?" she asked.

"Oh, yes. Yes. He's a gentleman. And she, the one he went with downstairs, she . . . Lady, too."

Miss Unwin saw then in her mind's eye that strangely well-furnished bedroom she had glimpsed once down below. And she thought she knew now why it was so well furnished in this shabby house. It was a place of assignation. The mysterious Mr. Sutter must have used it to meet a lady. And . . . In all probability, this was the secret about him that Alfie Goode had learnt. Only who was Mr. Sutter?

"Mrs. Burch," she asked again, "do you not know anything about this man who came here in the night? Nothing more than the sound of his voice?"

"Nothing. Nothing."

And, though she stayed with the old woman for almost another hour, she could get no more out of her.

At the end of that time she heard below the *click-click* on the stone floor of a countrywoman's wooden pattens, and, going down, she found that a neighbour's wife, hearing the news, had walked the mile or so from her cottage to look after the bereaved old woman. Gratefully, she handed over the care of her and left in company with Mr. Heavitree.

They discussed, as he drove her back to the Rising Sun, both her new discovery and the impasse it seemed to have led to. Mr. Heavitree was unable to recall anyone of the name of Sutter in the district, but they agreed that Miss Unwin should ask Mrs. Steadman whether she knew of anyone, perhaps a recluse hardly showing himself to the world.

"You know, my dear," Mr. Heavitree said as he halted in front of the inn to let Miss Unwin down, "if what old Mrs. Burch has told you is in any way true, then who is more likely to be the lady this mysterious Sutter met at the cottage than . . . Mrs. De Lyall?"

"Yes. Mrs. De Lyall. You may very well be right."

"It's worth some looking into," Mr. Heavitree said. "And I mean to drive straight over to her place to see what I can turn up."

"But you'll come back here as soon as you can and let me know what you've learnt?"

"I will, of course. But delicate inquiries of this sort take time, you know."

"Yes, I realise that. But when you return, I may have news of my own, too. Not about Mr. Sutter, whom I begin to suspect perhaps of going under an alias, but from Vilkins. Vilkins may have completed her inquiries at the War Office."

Mr. Heavitree smiled slowly. "You know," he said, "I'd give a sovereign to be hiding somewhere by when that young woman talks to the clerks she finds there."

Miss Unwin managed to laugh, and bade the old detective goodbye and good hunting.

She entered the inn and went up to her bedroom to refresh herself after the trials of the morning. But she had hardly taken off her bonnet when, from Mrs. Steadman's sitting-room immediately below, there came the sounds, one after another, of piercing, shrill, terrified screams.

15

Miss Unwin did not hesitate. She dropped her bonnet on the floor, ran to the door, flung it open, raced down the narrow stairs from the attics, tore over to Mrs. Steadman's sitting-room, and jerked its door wide.

An astonishing sight met her eyes.

Betsey, big and bouncing, was standing hard up against the wall of the room beside the fireplace with its paper ornament in the grate. Her normally cherry-red cheeks were a shade of dull grey, and she looked as if she wished she could fall backwards through the very wall behind her.

And, standing facing her, taut as an anchor-cable, was little Mrs. Steadman. Had not the attitudes of the two of them been so tense, they would have seemed comic. Betsey, tall and splendidly built, frozen in fear, and Mrs. Steadman, her head a good fifteen inches below the maid's, her diminutive figure quite dwarfed, nevertheless menacing her completely.

As well she might do, Miss Unwin realised, suddenly seeing in her hand the gleaming, pointed blade of a black-handled kitchen knife.

She stepped forward, came up beside the transfixed pair, and put her own hand on Mrs. Steadman's sinewy bare forearm.

"What—what is this?" she asked.

The few words were enough. All the taut force went out of Mrs. Steadman's tiny frame. The black-handled knife dropped to the floor.

"She—she knows. She knows something," she said, her voice hardly more than a whisper.

Miss Unwin gave Betsey a quick look. The colour was flooding back into the girl's face. And with it there was, plain to see, a look of shame.

"Yes, Betsey," Miss Unwin said, "you do know something. Something about Mr. Steadman, isn't it?"

"Oh, miss."

"Yes, it's been at the back of my mind ever since I first set eyes on you that you were not quite easy in my presence, and I see now it was the thought that I was here to prove Mr. Steadman innocent that made you so. Well, hadn't you better tell us everything straight out now? I cannot believe that what you have to tell will be all that grave. You're a good girl, and if you had known anything that would have absolutely saved your master, you'd have spoken up before this. But now is the time to tell us whatever it is you do know, grave or petty."

"Yes, miss, yes. I wanted to, truly. Only it didn't seem . . . And then it was, well, private, like."

"I dare say. But tell us everything now. Private or not. It has to come out."

"Oh, yes, miss, I will, I will. It was just this. Well, Farmer Burch . . . Well, he fancied I, like. He's a gruff, shy sort of a man, miss, and didn't like to be seen a-courting a girl. But he liked me, and he found his chance to tell me."

"Nothing wrong in that, my dear," Miss Unwin said, thinking to herself that before much longer poor Betsey would have to learn that the man who had come courting her was now dead.

"No, nothing wrong," Betsey answered. "And I weren't going to have nothing wrong neither, though I dare say he'd have been ready if I was willing."

"But you were not. So go on."

"Well, he did promise to marry I. But— Well, he said as he

couldn't afford to keep a wife, not when he had his rent unpaid and other debts beside."

"Go on," Miss Unwin said again.

Thoughts were piling up in her head, but she thrust them aside until she had heard Betsey's story to the full.

"Well, I told him as I'd wait," Betsey went on. "He were worth waiting for, so I thought. A farmer, even if he were only a tenant and behind with his rent. But if he could get clear, why, then I'd be a farmer's wife, gruff though he might be."

"But you have not told me what you were keeping secret, have you?" Miss Unwin said.

Betsey hung her head. "No. No, but I will. I meant to make a clean breast on it, only when I began to say summat to the mistress just now, her went for me with that knife."

"Well, never mind about that. Tell us what it is now."

"Why, that one day not above a month ago Mr. Burch come to me and says he were ready to marry me right off. So I asked him as if he'd got the money for his back rent and all, and he said as he had. First off, I was rejoicing, like. But then I got to think."

"About how he had got that money, and how, just before, he had given evidence against Mr. Steadman, evidence that Mr. Steadman had said wasn't so?" Miss Unwin asked.

"Why, yes, miss. Yes, you gone and guessed it. And—and when Mary Vilkins told I you was come to find out the truth of it all, why, then I wanted to tell what I feared all the more. But I daresent, not if I still wanted to marry him, and I didn't know whether I did that or not. But just now when I saw the mistress a-weeping, the first time as ever I did, I began to tell all. Only she—"

"Yes, yes," Miss Unwin broke in then. "Well, what you had to say in the end was not so important. Yet it does put another brick in the building I am beginning to build, and you'd have done well to say it all earlier, my girl."

"Oh, miss. Oh, I'm sorry, I am. Right sorry."

And Betsey broke into floods of streaming tears, while at the same time Mrs. Steadman, who had collapsed onto the sofa, began babbling apologies.

Miss Unwin went over and did her best to reassure her.

"My dear, I know how desperate with worry you must be, and what you did was quite natural. But, remember, what I was just saying is quite true. Brick by brick the case against that unknown man is building up. Indeed, it is possible that I already know his name."

Mrs. Steadman jumped from the sofa, once more ramrod-stiff as any soldier from the Crimea campaign.

"Who is he? Where can I find him?"

Miss Unwin put a soothing hand on her arm. "Don't hope too much," she said. "Don't hope too much."

"But you say you have his name?"

"Well, does the name Sutter mean anything to you?"

"Sutter? Sutter? But I don't know any Sutter."

The little spark of hope in Miss Unwin's head, which she had done her best to keep down, died then.

"No," she said, "I feared as much. Sutter must be an alias. The man who uses it had good reason to keep himself as much in the dark as he could."

Then, after the blubbering Betsey had been sent sharply about her work, Miss Unwin told Mrs. Steadman all that had happened out at Arthur Burch's farm. But the landlady, rack her brains as she might, was unable to recall anyone, near or far, with a name even at all like Sutter.

"No, my dear," she concluded after they had been going over it all for more than an hour, "it's no use. We're as far from it as ever. Jack, my poor Jack, will hang come Friday. I know he will."

Miss Unwin sighed. "Perhaps you do well not to hope. But I must hope myself. I must believe that, somehow, before that time on Friday morning, I can, with Mr. Heavitree's help, and with Vilkins's, find not only the man who played this foul trick on your husband but proof, too, that he did it."

"But won't the name be enough?"

"No, I'm afraid it hardly will. Not when the Home Secretary himself has already been appealed to and has decided against."

Mrs. Steadman bit her lip. "Oh, and to think," she said, "when General Pastell told me he was getting up a petition, I blessed him. I blessed him, and now you tell me that, because the Home Secretary has made up his mind, not even naming the true villain will save my Jack."

"I would be bringing you false comfort if I said anything else," Miss Unwin replied. "No, what I must be able to do is to go to the Chief Constable with such strong proof that he will have no choice but to telegraph the Home Secretary himself. No message coming from any other but a Chief Constable will serve, I fear."

She sat then in the neat little sitting-room with Mrs. Steadman while the hours of the day passed slowly on. There was nothing, she felt, that she could do now. Her only hopes lay in, first, what Mr. Heavitree might ferret out about Mrs. De Lyall and the lover they suspected she had met at Arthur Burch's miserable farm, and, second, in Vilkins. In Vilkins, who quite possibly had not been able to find a single clerk coming out of the War Office to the nearby public houses who would agree to help her with the list of names she had taken up to London.

When it had got well into the afternoon, Miss Unwin began to look out for Mr. Heavitree. Each time she heard from the sleepy road the clop of horses' hooves she went to the window. Mrs. De Lyall's mansion lay some ten miles from the town, she understood, and it ought not to take the good horse in Mr. Heavitree's hired trap very long to cover the distance.

But what might he not have had to do in the immediate vicinity of the house? He could not go and question Mrs. De Lyall directly. Indeed, she doubted if it would be possible for him to obtain an interview with her on any pretext. No, he would have to go round and round, getting into conversation

with anyone who seemed likely to be able to tell him anything about the lady.

And then, too, he would have had to take care that Captain
Brackham, living at the wretched inn nearby, did not get to
hear of his activities. It might be very late in the day before
the old detective had anything in the way of news to bring
her.

There was, too, Mrs. De Lyall's threat to herself to be
thought about. Last night it had not been her burly footmen
who had come up the path beside the house to give her the
beating that had been promised, and nothing had been seen
of them today, but this did not mean that Mrs. De Lyall's
threat had been wholly idle. At any time now it could be
carried out. She had been warned.

Yet perhaps Mr. Heavitree would have news about this,
too.

So it was with a bound of delight that, only at the fourth
time she had jumped to her feet and hurried to the window,
she saw the familiar trap coming down the road.

It was not, however, till she had been looking at it for
perhaps half a minute that she realised there was something
different about it. The figure in the driving seat was not Mr.
Heavitree's. In place of the old detective's tweed suit and
brown billycock hat, the driver wore, she saw now, the smock
of a countryman and had on his head an old straw.

She pushed herself farther out the window and looked
hard at the approaching vehicle. But there could be no
doubt. It was the one in which she had travelled that morning to Farmer Burch's cottage. Painted a dark green, like
many another trap of its sort, its owner had for some reason
or another added a band of bright orange all round its top.
She had thought, that morning, that the colour was unpleas-
antly garish.

So why was this other man driving it? And where was Mr.
Heavitree?

With hardly a rapid excuse to Mrs. Steadman, she left her

place at the window, ran downstairs and, bonnetless, out into the road.

The trap was just drawing abreast of the inn. When its driver saw her, he brought the horse—Yes, Miss Unwin thought, it is just the chestnut we had—to a halt.

"Would you be a Miss Unwin?" he asked in a twanging Oxfordshire accent, taking out of his mouth the clay pipe he had been sucking at.

"Yes, I am Miss Unwin. But Mr. Heavitree, where is he? Has anything happened to him?"

"Why, yes, you've the right on that," the man answered, the slowness of his speech filling her with irritation.

"What? What, for heaven's sake, has happened?"

"Why, he be hurt."

"Hurt? Hurt? How? Is he seriously injured? He's not dead, is he?"

"Oh, ah, no. Not dead. No, not dead at all. The surgeon do be saying as he'll be on his feet again come a fortnight."

"On his feet? In a fortnight? Whatever has happened? For heaven's sake, tell me everything."

"He be in a fight," the man said, slow as ever. "Leastways, he be as well knocked about as if he been."

"A fight? Who knocked him about?"

"Ah, that's easy to tell. It were that Captain Brackham, none other."

Miss Unwin felt she was beginning to understand. She went up to the trap and stood holding its orange-painted side.

"Now," she said, "tell me everything. Take your time, but tell me every single thing you know about it all."

"Ah." The man in the smock leant away to have a healthy spit over the far side of the trap. "It were like this," he said. "Mr. Heavitree, for such I understand be the gentleman's name, came to the inn where I sometimes gives a hand in the stable, the Fox and Hounds. He were asking all sorts of questions, mostly about that Mrs. De Lyall up at the Grange. And then someone goes and tells him if he wants to know any-thing about her, he might as well ask Captain Brackham who's been staying at the Fox for many a week and knows that Mrs. De Lyall well. Only, they say, he'd better stir his-self, since the Captain be just leaving, and him in a blessed hurry, too."

"Leaving?" Miss Unwin was unable to stop herself ex-claiming.

"Now, weren't I telling you just that? Leaving, I said, leav-ing, and in a fine hurry. And so this Mr. Heavitree o' yourn goes traipsing round to the yard where the Captain be just getting into his carriage, one o' they fast 'uns with a pair o' fine horses in the shafts. A curridgle, I think they calls 'em."

"A curricle, a curricle."

"Well, if that's how you likes to say it. But as I was a-telling you, only you broke in, into this curridgle the Captain was getting, and Mr. Heavitree comes up to him like and says as he wants a word. But Captain he bain't ready to give him a word, it seems, and what you might call a argumenty broke out. Then, afore you knows it, the Captain was a-striking out at your friend and left him on the ground with a mort o' broken ribs, so they say, and summat worse as well."

"But the surgeon thinks he will be up in a fortnight?"

"Oh, aye. He bain't hurt so very bad, though he do be fallen into insenserberry now. But afore he went, he rose up and begged that they let a Miss Unwin o' the Rising Sun in Compton know. And so here be I, sent all this way for 'ee, and few thanks I get."

"No, no," Miss Unwin assured him. "I do thank you. I thank you indeed. I have not my purse by me, but if you will wait . . ."

Her effusiveness changed the old countryman's attitude.

"No, no. I want no money for a Chrissen act," he said. "And besides, I'm to be paid proper for a-taking the trap back to where it was hired. So I'll bid 'ee good day."

And with a cheerful crack of his whip the fellow turned the trap and made off up the road.

Miss Unwin went back towards the inn. But, walking slowly and thoughtfully in the warm afternoon sun, she had not reached its doorway when her attention was caught by the sounds of horses' hooves beating a rapid tattoo on the dusty surface of the road behind her.

Had the old countryman forgotten some important message from Mr. Heavitree?

She turned, realising as she did so that the sound of the hooves had been much louder and faster than those of the horse in the hired trap.

And, coming in a cloud of rising dust towards her, she saw, once again, Mrs. De Lyall's canary-yellow phaeton with its two tall, stone-faced footmen up on the back. They had not come at nightfall yesterday. Were they here to do their vicious work now?

16

Mrs. De Lyall's two fine roans were pulled up in a rearing halt, sending the dust of the road rising in a swirling cloud. Mrs. De Lyall's coachman sat in his high seat, solid as a pillar of stone, as if the wild canter and the sudden dramatic halt had been none of his doing. Mrs. De Lyall's two tall, black-browed footmen stood behind her as she sat in the open phaeton, still as a pair of carefully matched statues apparently altogether oblivious of Miss Unwin outside the Rising Sun with the dust slowly settling on her bonnetless head.

Mrs. De Lyall raised her veil. "So, my madam," she said without preliminary, "I find you still in the town."

"I have business here," Miss Unwin answered, with equal curtness.

Mrs. De Lyall's eyes flashed. "Yes," she said, "and it is business that I do not care to have disturbing myself and my neighbours."

"I am sorry for that. But when it is a question of a man's life, then if there is disturbance, it must be endured. No matter by whom."

An angry flush darkened the rouge on Mrs. De Lyall's cheeks.

"Yesterday," she said, "I took the trouble to warn you, my fine miss, just what would happen to you if you persisted in staying here."

"You did. And night fell. And I am here still." Miss Unwin drew herself up and looked straight at her antagonist in the carriage.

"You know, do you not, that I have only to nod my head

and those two fellows at my back will be down on the ground and dealing with you in an instant."

"I think not."

"You do? Why, I have half a mind to show you otherwise."

"In a public road? Ordering your servants to disturb the Queen's peace?"

"Yes, madam. That. Do you think that in the county here any policeman would dare interfere, when I am acting in the interests of all my neighbours, magistrates and gentlemen?"

Mrs. Unwin thought then that Mrs. De Lyall's threats, extravagant though they seemed, might not be altogether airy nothings. The lady might be looked down on by her gentlemanly neighbours, but there could scarcely be one of them not susceptible to her flaunted beauty. She herself had seen as much at General Pastell's ball. She had seen a man as kindly and correct as the General himself succumbing to those lures.

But she could not back down now.

"If need be, madam," she said, as loudly and clearly as she could make herself speak, "I shall have to put your threats— for that is what they are—to the test."

"You refuse to pack your bags and go?"

"I have said I have business in the town, and in the neighbourhood. Business on which a man's life depends. I am not going to leave at your behest."

Mrs. De Lyall was positively dark with anger now under the careful layer of rouge.

"Not at my behest, you insolent creature?" she said. "Then let us see whether you will go at the behest of the authorities. Heaven knows, there is little love lost indeed between myself and Major Charteris, the Chief Constable of the county. But I think, were I to go to him, he would have no difficulty in choosing between a landowner and a slut from London."

That "slut" hurt Miss Unwin. When, later, she thought about the encounter, she realised that it was the tiny sliver of truth in the jibe that had made her momentarily so furious that she had been unable to speak. Certainly she was no slut, nor had she any inclination to behave as a slut. But she knew that many girls brought up as she had been, in the very lowest reaches of society, were left with no choice but to take to the life of a slut so as to have bread to eat. The gifts she herself had inherited from either one or other of her unknown parents or perhaps from both—her sense of logic, her intelligence, and her determined ambition—had saved her from that life. But she felt that there but for the grace of God she went. And the word hit her like a whip stroke.

Yet she forced herself to recover from it.

"Very well, madam," she said. "If going to the Chief Constable is what you have a mind to do, then do it. And I will trust that I in my turn shall be able to persuade the gentleman to act as justice dictates."

"Coachman, drive on."

Miss Unwin heard the words with an inner gratitude for the deliverance they brought. She found it hard not to let it appear at once on her face. But not a trace of it did she allow to surface until the canary-yellow phaeton was well up at the other end of the road. Then she let the tears she had forced back break out, careless of who might see her.

At last, limp with exhaustion, she managed to get back inside the inn.

In the cool darkness she stood, finally recovering herself. Taking a long deep breath, she forced her good logical mind to go over every word and gesture of that upsetting incident. And, as at last she set foot on the stairs to go up to Mrs. Steadman, she came to a decision.

She would have to go very soon to Major Charteris. It was necessary now to confront him face-to-face.

She wished with all her heart that she had old Mr. Heavitree there to consult. Now, if ever, she needed his experience. But there was no time to waste in hiring a conveyance and making the long journey to the wretched public house near Mrs. De Lyall's mansion in the hope that the old detective might have regained consciousness.

And, besides, firm though she was in her decision not to be frightened away by Mrs. De Lyall's threats, it would be the height of foolishness, she felt, deliberately to go to within a short distance of where she lived. Those two tall footmen had remained statue-still during the angry confrontation down in the road outside. But they could easily have been unleashed, and if they had been, she had little doubt they would have inflicted sharp physical harm.

So, instead of continuing to sit with Mrs. Steadman and wait for the slender chance of Vilkins's return with some useful indications from the War Office clerks, she told the landlady that she was sorry but would have to leave her for a while.

Then she took her bonnet and her parasol and, following Mrs. Steadman's directions, hired at the railway station a fly to take her to Major Charteris's house.

Sitting in the decrepit vehicle, which was all that was to be had, with an equally decrepit horse and an even more decrepit fly-man, she had plenty of time to ponder what she would say to the Major when she met him again.

She hoped that her swift deduction of the morning about the manner of Arthur Burch's death would stand her in good stead. The Chief Constable, surely, must acknowledge that she was not the simple, silly woman he had put her down as when he had first stepped into the death chamber at the farm. But time had passed since then, and he would perhaps have begun to discount the startling proof she had been able to give that Arthur Burch's death was murder.

So, now would the Major treat her, not altogether as a helpless female, but as someone not worthy of much consideration?

The wretched horse jogged on along the road, straggling across the slope of the Valley of Death, came to a stop, seized with feeble teeth a tussock of grass from the roadside, was half-heartedly cursed by the fly-man, and at last slowly dragged the fly on its way once more.

No, Miss Unwin decided, she would not say a word to the Chief Constable about Mrs. De Lyall and her threat. To do so would seem to show herself as weak as Major Charteris, that Tartar hero, would expect her to be. Instead she would confine her conversation with him strictly to Arthur Burch's murder. Tell him she must now that she was here to find who had killed Alfie Goode. But beyond that she would not go.

The fly suddenly dipped and swerved. Its ancient horse had attempted to shy, startled by a cock pheasant whirring up from under the wayside hedge.

Miss Unwin, recovering, looked at the watch pinned to her dress and wondered how much longer the journey would take. Major Charteris lived, so Mrs. Steadman had said, in a new house he had built for himself when he had gained his present office after retiring from the Army. The small estate that went with it incorporated at its edge Arthur Burch's ill-kept farm and cottage. Thus, it should not be all that far from Chipping Compton, not if she herself had been able to walk to the cottage.

So why was this journey, even with the wreck of a horse, taking so long?

As if in answer to her unspoken question, the fly-man turned in his seat, pointed with his whip—Miss Unwin saw, with amusement, that even this was a hopelessly frayed affair —and broke into surly speech.

"That be the house, through them trees. Right at the top of the hill. Must you go all the way?"

Miss Unwin was tempted to answer that she had already agreed to the fare and should be taken to her destination to the last yard. But the thought of getting out of the dilapidated vehicle and being free to go at her own determined pace kept her silent.

"Very well," she said. "Wait here. I will walk."

She pushed open the door of the fly—it stuck—and got

down. The day was still hot and the sun struck directly onto the lane. But she put up her parasol and marched firmly off.

Nevertheless, by the time she got to the door of Major Charteris's new grey stone house, all turrets and arched windows, she knew that she was not looking her best. Her face, she was certain, must be very red, if not sweat-streaked. And she had an acute longing for a glass of cool water.

But she would not let herself delay and reached forward and gave the big bell-pull a determined tug. Were she to spend time preparing herself for the interview ahead, she knew, she might very well lose heart.

A pretty, pert maidservant in a lavender dress and white cap and apron answered her ring.

"Is Major Charteris at home?"

The maid looked her up and down. "The Major's at home," she said, "But he don't see just anyone as comes to call. You got a visiting card?"

Miss Unwin cursed herself for lacking this essential instrument for polite visiting. But then her visit was not one of politeness.

"Will you tell the Chief Constable," she said, "that Miss Harriet Unwin, whom he met at Mr. Burch's farm early this morning, wishes to see him on a matter of urgent business?"

The girl seemed quelled by the firmness of that. With an assurance that she would deliver the message, she invited Miss Unwin to wait in the hall.

Indoors it was delightfully cool after the walk up the steepness of the hill. Miss Unwin was not unhappy to wait for as long as the Major kept her.

She looked round. The house had evidently been built to take full advantage of a taste for the ancient and monastic, which seemed odd in a retired military man. A long, narrow stained-glass window sent a chequered light onto the wide oaken-planked floor. The doors leading out of the hall were deeply panelled, and each was framed in a pointed arch. The newel-post of the stairs leading to the upper floors was in the shape of a bald monk's head.

It came to Miss Unwin at last as she waited that the man she was here to see must be desperately concerned to establish his respectability. No doubt, she realised, he had been one of those Army officers who had not had the wealth or family connections to purchase, stage by stage, his promotions. He must have had to wait for years as a lieutenant, then as a captain, and at last as a major while young men of good family and few abilities rose up over him to command regiments.

No wonder he had a reputation for insisting on the utmost rigours of discipline. What was it that Inspector Whatmough had said to Mr. Heavitree? *All shouted orders and parades and marching.*

A man like that would hardly be inclined to break with tradition and give a female detective, or, worse, a mere governess passing as a female detective, much of a hearing.

The pert maid came clattering down the wide wooden stairs.

"The Major will see you now," she said.

Miss Unwin followed her up the stairs—it was plain she was deliberately setting a cracking pace—along a wide corridor hung with undecipherable paintings of respectable country views, up another narrower twisting staircase to the single door at its head.

The maid opened it and popped her head inside.

"The lady that called," she said with more familiarity than Miss Unwin thought proper.

She remembered the pale woman with the headache who had asked her for a composing draught at General Pastell's ball. That had been Major Charteris's wife. So, did the Major like to have pretty and pert maidservants in his house, and let them be rather more familiar than maids ought to be? If it was so, then his attitude to herself was likely to be all the more contemptuously masculine.

"Come in," a voice barked from the other side of the door.

Miss Unwin entered. She found herself in a circular room, evidently the top floor of the most imposing of the turrets of the house. At the far side, in front of a wide window, its panes diamond-shaped and framed in lead, stood a large desk, at which the Chief Constable sat, as if secure within a redoubt defending Sebastopol, an intransigent Russian. Round the walls here, now emphasising the Major's military past, were hung crossed sabres, banners, and ancient muskets.

Miss Unwin advanced unhesitatingly under the fire of the Chief Constable's fixed glare.

"Well, madam," he said when at last she reached the desk, "what can I do for you?"

There was a chair beside the desk, tall-backed and with a hard horsehair seat. Though she had not been invited to sit, Miss Unwin took it. Then, placing the point of her closed parasol neatly between her feet and leaning slightly forward with her hands crossed on its handle, she addressed the man she knew she had to win over.

"Major Charteris, I will come straight to business. When we met this morning, I did not have an opportunity of telling you what was the purpose of my visit to Arthur Burch."

"A lady magazine writer," Major Charteris said dismissively. "Had the curiosity to inquire of my Inspector What-mough."

"But you were misinformed," Miss Unwin said.

The Major jerked up in his chair.

"Yes, misinformed, sir. I have come to Chipping Compton to rectify a gross injustice. John Steadman, who is to be hanged on Friday for the murder of Alfred Goode, is not guilty of that crime. And I am here to find the man who is."

There was a grim silence.

Miss Unwin wondered whether the Major was not about to slam a large red hand down on the domed brass bell she saw on his desk and request his pert parlourmaid to escort her from the building.

17

The Chief Constable's hand remained, however, where it was, laid flat and squarely on the leather-topped surface of his big desk. And, after letting the brooding silence go on for what seemed to Miss Unwin many minutes, he spoke.

"You are aware, madam, that the man Steadman was investigated by members of my own force, notably Inspector Whatmough, under my close personal supervision?"

"I had supposed as much, sir."

Miss Unwin hesitated. Then she rushed on. "But the best of us can make mistakes, sir. When I was asked to look into this business myself, I will confess that after I had studied the particulars, it seemed to me almost certain Mr. Steadman had indeed killed Alfred Goode."

"And it seems to me still quite certain."

"But, sir—"

"And you say you were asked to look into the matter. Who was it who asked you?"

Miss Unwin's spirits sank. How could she say to the Chief Constable of the county that she, a mere governess, had been asked to investigate the case his men had declared open-and-shut by, of all people, a housemaid?

She bit her lip. "I am afraid, sir, I am not at liberty to divulge that without the prior permission of my principal."

"Hm."

But the Chief Constable's grunt seemed to be an acknowledgement. Evidently he respected a "principal" of such social importance that permission had to be sought before the name could be disclosed. Miss Unwin thanked her lucky stars that she had by chance replied to the Major's query in such high-sounding terms.

"Sir," she began again, feeling bolder, "let me continue. When, as I say, I first looked into the case, it appeared to me that John Steadman must be guilty. But, after taking into consideration certain factors not available to Inspector Whatmough, I decided the matter was worth at least some further inquiry."

Again she trusted that fine words would conceal from the Major that the "certain factors" unknown to Inspector Whatmough had been no more than the fervent belief of the accused man's wife that he could not have killed anyone in a cowardly fashion, backed up by a handful of character references from such persons as a midwife and the town beadle.

"And what were the results of these further inquiries you were pleased to make, madam? What results did you achieve? If any?"

"A sad result indeed, sir. The death at someone else's hands of Arthur Burch."

The Chief Constable sat back with a sharp jerk.

"You connect Burch's murder with the other affair?" he said slowly.

"Of course, sir. I had talked to him about the evidence he gave at the assizes. Mr. Heavitree, who is known to you and who has agreed to assist me, had also questioned him. We both came to the conclusion that he lied in that evidence, and that he was beginning to be unhappy at having done so. This morning when you met us we had gone to the farm in order finally to persuade him to admit his error, something we were convinced that he would do."

"I see. And you believe that whoever it was who killed Burch got there before you?"

"That would appear to be the logic of the matter."

"Logic, eh?"

The Chief Constable darted her a sceptical look from under his shaggy eyebrows. Logic, from a woman.

"Yes, sir, logic," Miss Unwin answered firmly. "I do not think that you will be able to fault it."

Major Charteris did not take up the challenge.

"Well," he said, "I grant that there may seem to be a case for linking these two affairs. But let me tell you that what you have alleged is by no means proved. Who do you think murdered Burch? Can you put a name at all to the man?"

"Yes, sir. I can."

Miss Unwin saw Major Charteris's large hands grip the edge of the desk in front of him.

"But, sir," she said hastily, "it is no discredit to you or your men that I can do so. And the name I can give you is, I am almost certain, only an alias."

"An alias?"

"Yes, sir. I comforted old Mrs. Burch during a period of nearly two hours after her son's death, and she eventually gave me particulars she had been afraid to disclose to anyone earlier."

"And these particulars were . . . ?"

"That for some time past a man and a woman, a gentleman and a lady whom she had never seen, had been meeting in secret at night in the cottage. They had even furnished a bedroom for themselves there."

"And you believe this old woman's tale?"

"She told me not a little about the circumstances, sir, and I did not detect any inconsistencies in her account."

"Hm?"

The Major grunted again. But this time there was a good deal more doubt in the sound.

"And you say she gave you a name?" he asked. "Was it the gentleman's, if gentleman there was, or the lady's?"

"It was the gentleman's. The name was Sutter."

"Sutter? Sutter? I can recall no one of that name in the county."

"No, and none of the inquiries I have made have produced anyone of that name either."

"So, what you have been telling me is a heap of suppositions."

"Suppositions backed by firm evidence. There could scarcely be any evidence firmer than that dead body you and I saw this morning."

"I dare say."

"So, sir, this is what I have come to you to request: the full assistance of the men of your force in running to earth the man who masquerades under the name of Sutter. Their utmost exertions."

The Chief Constable sat and pondered.

"You know that what you are asking is that public servants should spend time and money attempting to show that a man who has been tried for murder and found guilty, a man whose appeal the Home Secretary himself has rejected, is not guilty of the crime for which he is to be hanged on Friday."

"It is because he is to be hanged then that I am requesting your assistance."

The Chief Constable gave a grunt of stifled irritation, or worse.

"Very well," he said, "I shall order Inspector Whatmough to make inquiries to discover who your mysterious Mr. Sutter may be. I shall press him to do his utmost. There you are."

Miss Unwin rose from her hard horsehair chair. "Thank you, sir," she said.

She thought it wise to leave as soon as the promise was hers. Further questions from the Major were to be avoided. The last thing she wanted was for him to learn that she was no more than a governess. If he came to know that, perhaps the firmness he had shown in giving her his pledge would melt away. And if she was forced to go farther and tell him that the governess's assistant investigator was her good friend, Vilkins, at this moment engaged in wheedling information illegally out of clerks from the War Office, all hopes of enlisting co-operation must instantly vanish.

"Good day to you, sir," she said.

And she left.

Walking back to where the feeble fly-man and his battered old fly waited, she began violently to wish that by the time they reached the Rising Sun she would find that Vilkins had got back. What if, when she scanned that list of military guests at General Pastell's ball, she found that somewhere at some time Jack Steadman had been in company with one of the officers on it? Then a hitherto hidden link might be revealed. Perhaps, too, it would become apparent why Jack Steadman had to die, even if it was through knowing something unknown to himself though brought to light by the mole-pryings of Alfie Goode.

She sat in the decrepit old fly—there was a large rent in the worn leather of its seat, and the stuffing was oozing out—and fretted with darting impatience every yard of the way. And the old horse was very much slower going home, climbing the steep slope at the other side of the Valley of Death, than it had been on the journey out.

At last, however, Chipping Compton came into sight. Again Miss Unwin abandoned the vehicle in favour of walking on her own two feet. She might not be able to go much faster than the wretched horse, but at least she would not try to halt at every tempting patch of grass.

She arrived at the inn. Without waiting to mount the stairs, she plunged into the kitchen behind the bars.

But there was no sign there of Vilkins.

So, toilingly at last, she went upstairs and looked into Mrs. Steadman's sitting-room. The little landlady was perched in her husband's big chair under the mantelpiece with its cheerful array of china dogs and bright fairground figures, looking as if she had not stirred from the position Miss Unwin had left her in more than two hours before.

"Mrs. Steadman," she exclaimed, "would you not be better perhaps in bed? I could send out for a sleeping draught. You ought to get some rest."

"With my man going to be killed on Friday morning?"

Miss Unwin stayed silent. There was no answer that could be made to those bitter words.

After a little, she thought of something which might at least rouse the landlady.

"While I was out," she said, "was there by any chance a further message about Mr. Heavitree? I am anxious, more than anxious, about him. It was on my behalf that he met with his injury."

"There may have been something downstairs," Mrs. Steadman answered. "I told them I wasn't to be worried. What does it matter to me now if there's a rough-house in the taproom, if the beer turns sour, if there's a fire. My life is over. Over. Or over it will be come Friday morning."

Once more Miss Unwin felt there was nothing to be said. She dared not give the poor creature any hope, even though in her mind she had now a strong glimmering of what might have happened in Hanger Wood. But unless she could take to the authorities clear proof, what she knew or guessed was so much dross. Jack Steadman would hang on Friday unless by then the real murderer had been shown beyond doubt to be who he was. To raise hopes that were so unlikely to be justified would be worse cruelty than remaining silent.

"I will go downstairs and ask," she said. "Perhaps someone has ridden over with news."

Serving in the private bar she found Betsey, seemingly not greatly affected by the death of the man she had hoped to marry for the small respectability it would have given her, and even looking the picture of rude health again with the burden on her conscience removed.

"Betsey," she said, "has there been a message at all about poor Mr. Heavitree?"

"Why, gracious, yes. I forgot all about 'un. There was a higgler coming our way with his cart—I bought a ribbon off him—and the landlord at the Fox and Hounds took pains especial to let us have word."

"And what did he say? Has Mr. Heavitree recovered consciousness? Or is he worse? Don't tell me the blow proved fatal."

"No. No, the poor fellow's no worse nor no better, it seems. But the surgeon has been with him again, and he holds out good hopes."

With that, Miss Unwin had to be content. But she dearly wished that she could have heard that the old detective had recovered consciousness. If he had, she thought, she might, late though the day was growing, set out to see him. She needed his advice more than ever. The affair was surely reaching crisis point.

But advice she was not going to get.

She sighed.

If anything was to be done, she would have to do it herself. And with no one to caution her if what she attempted proved more rash than it ought to be.

Lying in bed later, lying there but far from sleeping, she thought that in all probability next day she would have to take action, with Vilkins back or not, with particulars from the War Office she could use or without them.

Time was too short for anything else. Better to take a risk, even the boldest and most desperate risk, than to stay and watch the hands of the clock go round till they reached eight o'clock on Friday morning. Until the trap dropped beneath Jack Steadman, the hangman's rope round his neck.

Innocent and helpless Jack Steadman.

18

The early train from London reached Chipping Compton at eighteen minutes past ten in the morning, so Miss Unwin had learnt. But she found herself standing on the platform of the railway station a whole quarter of an hour before it was due, so sharp was her anxiety.

It was not even, she told herself, very likely that Vilkins would be on it. If she had succeeded the day before with the help of a clerk from the War Office in checking the careers of all the Army officers in the neighbourhood, General Pastell's ball-night guests, then she ought to have been in time to catch the last train of the day then and she would have reached Chipping Compton late at night. On the other hand, if she had not yet managed to find a clerk she could persuade to help, or if she still had to find out from one she had where some of the officers on the list had served, she would hardly have caught a train that left early in the morning.

But now that list, by giving her an inkling of how Jack Steadman could have learnt unbeknowingly the secret of a victim of blackmail, was perhaps the only thing that was going to save him from the hangman.

So Miss Unwin stood on the wooden platform, peering into the distance, from where, round a gentle bend in the line, the London train would come. It was quiet and still on yet another flawless summer's day. A few birds were singing in the elms beside the station and insects chirped and droned in the warm air. But beyond this there was scarcely a sound.

Miss Unwin leant on the handle of her parasol, its point between her feet, and craned to hear.

Then at last, like the distant rattle of musketry, there came a tiny mechanical sound. The London train.

Oh, let Vilkins be on it. Let Vilkins be on it, Miss Unwin prayed.

The noise of the approaching train grew louder, not musketry now but the thunder of cannon.

Into the Valley of Death, Miss Unwin thought.

Would the train's forward march bring as much success, despite all odds, as that cavalry charge of twenty and more years ago?

> Flashed all their sabres bare,
> Flashed as they turned in air,
> Sabring the gunners there,
> Charging an army, while
> All the world wondered:
> Plunged in the battery-smoke
> Right through the line they broke;
> Cossack and Russian
> Reeled from the sabre-stroke,
> Shattered and sundered.

She found she had all Mr. Tennyson's words there in her head.

With a furious screeching of brakes and wild hissing of steam, the locomotive drew up at the platform.

Miss Unwin looked left and right—*Cannon to the right of them, Cannon to the left of them*—along the length of the train. One door opened. Another.

From the first a stout gentleman stepped out, tall silk hat gleaming. The station's sole porter hurried up to him, touched his cap, and relieved him of a small attaché case. From the other opened door, that of a third-class carriage, there slowly emerged, back first, a boldly patterned green-and-yellow skirt. A hand holding a large basket covered with a red-checked cloth followed, and finally there came a fat farmer's wife.

Miss Unwin scanned the whole length of the train once more. Not a sign of another door being thrust open.

Well, she thought, it was really quite unlikely that Vilkins . . .

She heard the guard's long whistle-blast and turned to see him waving with heavy self-importance his large green flag. The locomotive emitted a whistle-blast of its own, deep and sustained.

And another third-class door was hurled wide. Stumbling from the already moving train, straw bonnet trailing by its ribbons, came Vilkins.

Miss Unwin ran forward to save her from falling headlong onto the platform.

She just managed it and brought her friend to an upright position, puffing and panting, her round face with its dab of a nose red as a post-box.

"Whatever happened?" she asked. "Why were you so late off the train?"

"Oh, oh. For 'eaven's sake, let me catch me breath."

Vilkins stood in the sun and panted. Miss Unwin went and retrieved her parasol, which she had had to fling aside when she had rushed to save her friend.

"Well, it's plain as a pikestaff, really," Vilkins said, still breathing heavily, as she returned.

"Is it, my dear?"

"Yeh. You see, there I was, up all night, all blooming night. An' try as I might in that train, jogging along like I was a babe in its cradle, I couldn't no more keep awake than what I could walk on a tightrope."

"And you were asleep when the train pulled in here? I see. But what is this about being up all night? You had money enough for a bed when you left here."

"Had to spend it, didn't I? Had to try some o' your old bribery an' corruption."

"But, Vilkins, who? Whom did you have to bribe? And—

and are you sure you will not be detected? And, Vilkins, were you successful?"

"Questions, questions. Jus' stand still, an' let me get meself sorted out."

"Yes, I'm sorry. You're only just awake and you had all the flurry of getting off the train before it swept you away. Let's go to the Rising Sun, and then you can tell me all about it."

"Yes. All right. But 'ow about you, Unwin? 'Ave you solved the murder while I been away?"

"Oh, my dear, no. No, for that I think I need what you have been able to get from the War Office. If you have got anything. And have you, my dear?"

"Oh, yes. Yes, I got the lot. Though it took me till late last night to do it. But ain't you got even one bit further on all the time I been in London?"

Miss Unwin paused at the wide open door of the Rising Sun. "Yes, my dear," she said. "I think—I suspect that I have got further, a good deal further. Only . . ."

"Only what, for 'eaven's sake?"

"Only what I think happened, what I suspect without having any real proof must have happened, is so . . . so extraordinary that I hardly dare tell even myself that it is so."

" 'Strawdinary? Well, it's 'strawdinary enough that poor Jack Steadman didn't do what everybody said 'e did do, with all what they call that evidence there in Hanger Wood agin him."

"Yes, you're right, my dear. In a way the very peculiarity of all that makes the extraordinary thing I believe must have happened more likely. Yes, much more likely."

"Well, then," Vilkins said, " 'oo done it? Out with it, Unwin."

"No," said Miss Unwin. "No, I cannot. It really is altogether too bizarre."

"Well, I don't know what bizarre is, 'less it's one o' them native markets in India or wherever it is. But I still can't see why you can't name a name. Straight I can't."

Miss Unwin gave her friend then a brief account of everything that had happened while she had been away in London, how with Mr. Heavitree she had tried to frighten Arthur Burch, how she had proved next morning that the farmer had been murdered, and how Mr. Heavitree had been attacked by Captain Brackham as the arrogantly reckless cavalryman was leaving the county with such unaccountable haste.

"But," she concluded, "perhaps when I have seen that list of yours and heard what the clerk from the War Office had to say about the officers on it, then I shall feel I have some confirmation, and then . . . then, Vilkins dear, I shall tell you that name."

"Well, come on up to Mrs. Steadman's parlour then, an' 'urry up about it."

In a minute more the two of them were in the landlady's sitting-room. Vilkins began pulling the list—it looked very tattered—from inside her blouse, where she must have put it for safety.

"You see," she explained, "I 'ad to tell the feller I got 'old of at the last that it was all being done for a bet. I mean, what else could I say? Seemed barmy asking 'im to find out about all them officers for no reason at all. An' then . . . Well, it all took time, see. An' 'e was beginning not to believe me. Don't know what 'e thought. Maybe that I was a blooming French spy, I don't know. So I 'ad to pretend that the feller making the bet—I said 'e was one o' the gentlemen in the 'ouse where I worked—I 'ad to pretend the bet was getting bigger an' bigger an' that the gent 'ad given me a yellowboy to pass on to 'im. Well, that did the trick all right."

"A sovereign," Miss Unwin said. "I should hope it did do the trick. And I suppose that was the pound you had for all your board and lodging in London?"

"In course it were. I didn' 'ave no other sovereigns, did I?"

"And that was why you had to spend the night without a bed?"

Vilkins burst out laughing. "You should of seen me," she said. "Trying to get a mite o' sleep perched up on a bit of a low wall. An' so uncomfortable I didn't stand a chance. Not that I could of, not with all them blokes what kept coming up to me an' asking."

"Oh, Vilkins."

"Yes, well, told 'em what they could do, didn't I? But then after a bit I 'ad to walk up an' down so's I could spot 'em coming an' go the other way."

"Oh, my dear. What I made you go through. But am I right in thinking it was worth it? You got all the postings of all the officers on that list?"

"Every last one."

"Then let me see. Let me see."

Miss Unwin almost snatched the crumpled piece of paper that the housekeeper at General Pastell's had given her— long ago, it seemed—and spread it out on Mrs. Steadman's round table. Then she drew towards her the old account-book in which the landlady had so carefully pasted every account of the inquest and her husband's trial.

She flipped through its bulky pages.

"Yes," she said. "Yes, here it is. What Mr. Serjeant Busfield said in mitigation, the account of Mr. Steadman's military career. Thank goodness the county paper printed every word of the trial."

"Well, they would of done, in course. Don't suppose anything so exciting's 'appened round 'ere since the beginning o' the blooming world."

"Well, it's a blessing for us at least. Now I can see whether any of these officers happened to be in the same place as Mr. Steadman at some time when something must have happened that gave Alfred Goode a chance of using the blackmail. Something, too, which would have given the chance to Mr. Steadman, were he that sort of a villain and had he but known he knew what he must have done."

"If you thinks I can foller all that, Unwin, you must 'ave a slate loose in the top storey, so you must."

"Well, never mind," Miss Unwin murmured absently, her head deep in the list of names with the War Office clerk's neat annotations against each one. His copperplate writing, monotonously regular, as might be expected of someone charged with copying document after document day after day, was not, in fact, easy to read. But Miss Unwin fought her way through it.

She tried to begin at the beginning. But hardly had she finished conscientiously checking each of the places beside the first entry than she could not stop herself flicking down to look at the one name on the list that had been in her head for all the past day.

And in a moment she saw that it fitted one particular period of Corporal Steadman's service—it was in the Crimea —down to the last detail.

So there is a link, she thought. And Alfie Goode had been a soldier, too, an Army farrier. It was more than possible that he had been there at the time as well. And something that had happened during the short period the three of them were all within the same small area must have given vicious Alfie Goode his hold. No doubt, he had been unable to take advantage of his knowledge until circumstances had, after a lapse of twenty years, unexpectedly brought him face-to-face with his victim here in the Valley of Death.

"You've found it." Vilkins's loud, almost accusing voice broke in on her thoughts.

She roused herself. "Yes, my dear," she said. "I've found what, I am all but certain, must be the link."

"Never mind your old links. 'Oo's the feller? That's what I want to know."

Miss Unwin put a finger against the name on General Pastell's housekeeper's list.

Vilkins bent over the sheet till her big blob of a nose was almost touching the paper. Miss Unwin could see her lips moving as she puzzled out the spelling. Then at last she looked up.

"So it ain't that Captain Brackham, arter all," she said. "An' I was certain sure it was going to be. Specially arter you a-telling me 'e'd skipped the blooming county."

"Ah, yes," Miss Unwin said. "But his doing that, I think, we owe to Mrs. De Lyall."

"The Spanishy one? But 'ow's she come into it?"

"Well, you told me that, in fact, when you told me what you'd overheard from the conservatory on the night of the ball."

"I said that was important. Vital, I said it was."

"Well, so in a way it was. It told me that Mrs. De Lyall was ready to go to great lengths to help the man who had killed Alfie Goode."

"Captain Brack— But you're saying it weren't 'im."

"No. You see, Vilkins, dear, I think you must have mistaken that voice you heard. You never actually saw the man talking with Mrs. De Lyall, did you?"

"No, but 'e come into the conservatory straightaway arter, that Captain Brackham."

"And that was what caused you to make your very natural mistake, my dear. No, Captain Brackham was never clever enough to plan this very clever murder. No more brains, my little friend Phemy Pastell said to me, than she had in her boot. He was only fit to be used by Mrs. De Lyall to create a kind of diversion."

"To throw you off the track, Unwin? But she ain't smart enough to do that, not 'er, she ain't."

"Well, she did not," Miss Unwin said.

And then she sat in silence, no longer seeing the list and its heavy covering of writing in the clerk's neat hand and Mrs. Perker's generous rounded one.

When she had thought with care for as long as five minutes, she turned again to Vilkins, standing steadily scratching behind her left ear.

"There's something I want you to do for me," she said.

"Just ask me."

"It's not difficult, but I'd rather you did it than I. I don't want to be put in the position of having questions put to me."

"Well, if they're put to me, that'll be all right. 'Cos I don't know any blinking answers."

"Yes, that's a decided advantage."

"All right, then. What's this I got to do?"

"It's to deliver a note I am about to write."

"I could do that all right, I 'ope. 'Oo's it to?"

"Why, to the Chief Constable, of course. Who else?"

"Well, if that's what you want," Vilkins said. "Just tell me where I can find 'is Majesty."

"I imagine he'll be at his house. I gather he spends most of his time there and expects Inspector Whatmough and his other officers to go out and see him. It's a place called Monkton Towers, on the other side of the Valley of Death."

"Far, is it? Will it take me long on me own two feet?"

"Well, it is a good long walk, my dear. But I'd rather you did go on foot. I don't want to make my note seem too urgent."

"Just as you like, Unwin. I don't mind walking, not 'owever far it is. Not in a good cause, like."

"Well, this is a good cause, dear. As good as ever there has been."

There was an inkwell and the wherewithal for writing on the mantelpiece, tucked behind the biggest china dog, and in a drawer underneath the table Miss Unwin found some sheets of letter-paper. She sharpened the quill pen she had found with the penknife that had been beside it and began to write, hardly hesitating now over the choice of her words.

"What you said, then?" Vilkins asked when she saw the note being signed. "That is, if you wants a girl to know."

"Oh, yes," Miss Unwin replied. "You don't think I would keep secrets from you, do you?"

"Only if you thought it was better for me to wallow in me ignorance."

Miss Unwin laughed. "No, I have never thought you were ignorant, my dear."

"All right, then, what you said?"

"Just this. *Dear Major Charteris, With reference to our conversation yesterday, I write now to let you know that I am able to ascertain the identity of the man who has gone under the name of Sutter. I remain, yours faithfully, Harriet Unwin.*"

"That ought to bring 'im running, if that's what you wants," Vilkins said.

"Yes, my dear, that's exactly what I want. And if all goes well, I begin to think now that poor Jack Steadman has a glimmer of hope, after all."

"'Ere, don't say it. It'll bring bad luck."

"Well, it might," Miss Unwin conceded as she lit a taper and melted some wax to seal her letter. "And it is only a glimmer. So don't let's either of us say a word more."

"Cross me 'eart," said Vilkins.

And she did. Only, Miss Unwin saw, she got the wrong side.

19

Miss Unwin knew that now she must simply wait with what patience she could for a response to her note to Major Charteris. There was little to be done in the interval. She did, however, as soon as Vilkins had set off, beg from Mrs. Steadman, now even less able to give attention to anything with her husband's death not as much as twenty-four hours away, a boy with the inn's tax-cart to go over to the Fox and Hounds to inquire how Mr. Heavitree was faring. She even accompanied the lad as far as the turning to Farmer Burch's cottage. Mrs. Burch, weeping and broken after her son's death, had been on her conscience.

"Gallows Corner," the boy said to her cheerfully as he set her down.

"Gallows Corner?"

"Aye, 'twas here they strung up the sheep-stealers and all, in the old days."

"Just here? Where the oak spreads all over the road?"

"Just here. Strung 'em up high as high."

Miss Unwin was unable to repress a shudder as she set off along the lane.

When she got to the ill-kept farm, she found the cottage deserted. She shrugged. No doubt the neighbour she had seen on the morning of the death had taken the old woman home with her.

She made her way back to the Rising Sun as quickly as she could.

The gruesomely inclined boy with the tax-cart returned from his errand not long after Vilkins had trudged back from the Chief Constable's. But the news about Mr. Heavitree was not what Miss Unwin had hoped for. He was still unconscious. The surgeon remained optimistic, however. It was, he had repeated, just a question of time. When his patient came to, he would soon be as good as ever.

But Miss Unwin knew time was not on her side.

She wanted nothing more than counsel, and the old detective was the only one who could give it to her. But if he was not there to help, he was not. She would have to act on her own—and trust that the risks she feared she would have to take did not bring disaster.

Oh, if only I had just one day more, she said to herself. Just one day. One day more.

But she did not have that extra day. Jack Steadman was to be hanged next morning.

Then at last, just after midday she had persuaded Mrs. Steadman to drink a little tea and eat some dry toast by way of dinner, she heard coming along the road—she had seldom been far away from the window that overlooked it—the sound of a trotting horse.

She wanted to run to the window, thrust it open, and lean right out. But she restrained herself. If this was, as she hoped, the Chief Constable himself coming to find out just how sound was her information about the mysterious Mr. Sutter, then too much eagerness on her part might well lose her the respect she had worked to gain.

But by the time the horse had reached the inn itself, standing well back from the window she was able to see that, yes, instead of sending Inspector Whatmough or any other policeman, the Chief Constable had come in person.

Hastily, she took Mrs. Steadman to her bedroom so that the interview between Major Charteris and herself could take place in privacy.

Hardly had she got back to the sitting-room than she heard steps on the stairs. Then Betsey, still looking infuriatingly well and unconcerned, put her head round the door.

"Miss, miss," she said. "It's—it's Major Charteris, and he do want to see you yourself and no other."

"Then let him come—"

But the door was thrust open and the Major himself strode in, riding whip in hand, heavy moustaches hanging ominously.

"Well, miss," he said, banging the door closed almost in Betsey's face, "what is this? You say you know who that Sutter fellow is. Let's hear."

"Ah, sir," Miss Unwin answered, forcing herself not to quail before this assault, "I fear you have misinterpreted my note."

"Misinterpreted? What the devil do you mean? It seemed clear enough to me. Short enough, too, for a female. But clear."

"I think you will find, sir," Miss Unwin replied, "that I said only that I had a good idea who our 'Mr. Sutter' is, not that I could give you his name."

"Same damn thing, ain't it?"

Miss Unwin would dearly have liked to rebuke the use of such language to a lady. But if she were simply the female detective she had allowed the Chief Constable to assume she was, then perhaps strong words of that sort were to be expected.

"Well, sir," she said, "it is not, if you will excuse me, quite the same thing. Perhaps my note, after all, was not as clear as it ought to have been. I meant only to say that I have been lucky enough to find a way in which the gentleman can be brought to book and seen for what he is, for who he may be."

"I trust, miss, you have not brought me riding all the way here on a damned wild-goose chase."

"Oh, I think not, sir. I know not, indeed."

"Well, then, suppose you explain yourself. *Try* to explain yourself, I should say."

"Very well, sir. You may well blame me for what I am about

to tell you, but after much consideration I find I can do nothing else."

"Damn it, woman, what's the fellow's name?"

"Sir, I believe I do know it. But—but, to tell the truth, it is so unbelievable that he . . . Well, sir, what I propose is this: I was out this morning at Farmer Burch's cottage again. I had gone there to see if all was well with his old mother, but I found that she had left."

"I dare say, I dare say. Very commendable, and all that. But what's your charitable disposition got to do with who murdered Burch?"

"Just this, sir. That while I was at the cottage I came upon something, an object. Sir, I am not even going to tell you what it was. But it indicated to me, almost beyond doubt, who was the man who had occupied that well-furnished bedroom at the cottage with a lady and who, I am quite certain, murdered Mr. Burch."

"Not tell me? Why the devil not? Listen to me, my fine miss, my patience with you is not very far from running out."

"I know it must be, sir. But nevertheless I ask you to trust me just a little further. That name— Sir, that name is to me incredible. But, sir, I am convinced that the person, the gentleman who left that tell-tale object at Farmer Burch's, will almost certainly go back for it. And he will go tonight. He cannot go very much longer without missing it, and as soon as he has realised it must be at the cottage, as he cannot have done before this, he is bound to attempt to retrieve it under cover of darkness.

"Retrieve it, eh?"

Into Major Charteris's somewhat bloodshot eyes there had come a look of sharp shrewdness.

"Yes, sir. And I venture to think that you have already understood what can be made of that. Sir, if you will instruct Inspector Whatmough to assemble a dozen of his best men and have them lie in wait in the darkness round the cottage, then our man will come walking into a trap. I am certain of it.

And I intend to be there myself in hiding, sir, to verify that he is who I believe him to be. Then, if my suspicions prove correct, if you would be so good as to supply me with a police rattle or a police whistle, I can spring the trap and the business will be done. In time to telegraph the Home Secretary, sir, and save John Steadman from the hangman's rope tomorrow morning."

Major Charteris stood looking down at her pensively, the riding whip in his right hand slapping rhythmically on his boot.

"Very well, then," he said at last. "I'll accept your conditions, Miss Unwin. Ridiculous though I believe them to be. But I make one condition of my own."

Miss Unwin felt the elation that had blazed up in her with the Chief Constable's agreement die suddenly away. To be replaced by an acute anxiety.

What would this condition be?

"On one condition," Major Charteris repeated.

"Yes, sir?"

"That I myself come with you to Burch's cottage tonight."

"You, sir?"

"Yes. You ask me to trust you. Well, I have agreed to do so. But trust goes just so far. I want to be there myself to see your famous Mr. Sutter come into the place exactly when you do. To see him with my own eyes."

"If that is what you insist upon."

"It is."

"Then, sir, let us meet, shall we say, an hour after sunset, at the cottage. And I will leave it to you to make all the arrangements with Inspector Whatmough. I hardly need emphasise, I am sure, that his men should be placed so that there is not the least chance of any intruder being frightened off."

"You can count on that, Miss Unwin."

Vilkins, when Miss Unwin told her what had been arranged, was outraged.

"Unwin," she said, "you ain't going to do it."

"My dear, I must. You must see that. I have explained the state of affairs. There is only this way to go about it. Remember, Jack Steadman dies at eight o'clock tomorrow morning unless the Home Secretary receives a full account by telegraph before then."

Vilkins's round face looked comically woebegone. "Well, all right," she said, "if you must you must. But I'm coming with you. That feller'll be dangerous. Mad killing dangerous."

"And I shall be prepared, my dear."

"Oh, Unwin, it ain't enough to be prepared. If you was going into a cage at the Zoo Gardens with a wild tiger, what good would it do you to be prepared?"

"Much more good than not to be prepared," Miss Unwin answered with her accustomed logic.

"Oh, don't give me that. I'm a-coming with you, I tell you."

"No, my dear, that would never do. Just think how it would seem to the Chief Constable if he found the female detective he has been persuaded, with great difficulty, to trust had come to their rendezvous with a housemaid beside her for protection."

"Don't care what he'd say," Vilkins answered. "I'd give 'im as good as 'e gave me. I dare swear I'd be better protection for you, Unwin, than one o' that man's policemen, yokels that they are. Why, you can't understan' more'n one word in a dozen what they says."

Miss Unwin smiled, little though she felt light-hearted. "No, my dear," she said, "I must go to that cottage tonight on my own. But there is one precaution I should like to take, one thing you can do for me."

"What's that, then?" Vilkins asked suspiciously.

It took Miss Unwin more than a little time to persuade her childhood friend and companion in adversity that what she proposed was, in fact, the only course open to her. But at last she succeeded.

20

When the long summer's day at last began to draw to its end, it was without anyone to accompany her that Miss Unwin set out from the Rising Sun for the rendezvous that would, she hoped with all her strength, lead to the saving of poor little Mrs. Steadman's husband. A deep-orange moon was beginning to rise as she tramped along, her light-grey alpaca dress covered with a large black shawl borrowed from the landlady.

She had wondered whether she should make an attempt to arm herself, if only with that kitchen knife with which Mrs. Steadman had threatened blustering, bouncing Betsey. But in the end she had come to the conclusion that no weapon would protect her if she was not quick enough when the time came.

Filled though she was with determination, she could not help slowing her steps as she approached the wide-spreading oak-tree where, the boy with the tax-cart had told her, the gallows had once stood. And at the edge of the patch of deep shadow beneath the tree, she found she had actually faltered to a complete halt.

Come, she told herself, I must not be ridiculous. There will be worse things to face by far before the night is out than a patch of darkness in the empty countryside.

She took a breath and marched forward.

From out of the deepest shadow a figure emerged, tall, menacing.

Miss Unwin gasped with fright.

"Miss Unwin, forgive me."

It was the familiar voice of Major Charteris, if unfamiliarly apologetic.

"I am sorry, miss, if I startled you. I thought it best to catch you at the lane-end rather than attempt to get into the cottage myself and wait for you there."

"Yes, you were quite right, sir," Miss Unwin answered, endeavouring to conceal her panting breath. "I ought to have suggested this afternoon that we met somewhere about here."

"Well, well, no harm done, eh?"

"None at all, sir. And let me congratulate you, while there is an opportunity, since I believe we should remain strictly silent so long as we are inside the house, on the skill your Inspector Whatmough has shown in concealing his ambush party. I saw not the least sign of them as I approached. I suppose they are indeed in place?"

The Major gave a grunt of a laugh. "Oh, yes," he said. "You can rely on an Army man to see that the military dispositions are correct. You need have no fear there. And may I congratulate you in having looked about you so carefully. If I had you under my command, I'd make a policeman of you yet."

Miss Unwin ignored the compliment. In a whisper she offered a last few suggestions for their vigil, and then they set off up the lane together. In silence.

They entered the cottage's neglected garden and, picking their way through the tall weeds and spiky ragged gooseberry bushes there, crept over to the door. The pungent smell of the unpicked fruit came sharply to Miss Unwin's nostrils.

"Shall we go in, then?" the Major murmured, pushing open the unlocked door.

Miss Unwin peered into the blackness inside, thick and forbidding. However, the kitchen door was half open, and through the low window on the far side of the dark room—it was where they had agreed to wait in hiding—the rising moon was casting some faint light.

Miss Unwin reasoned that, once they had grown accustomed to the gloom, they should be able to see well enough, even with the kitchen door closed.

She stepped forward and entered the room. The Major, coming in closely behind her, turned and carefully shut the rickety door.

In the darkness Miss Unwin became aware of the odour of stale food. She thought, too, that she could distinguish the sharper smell of busy mice.

She advanced quickly but cautiously farther in, making for the big table where that breakfast had been laid which had enabled her to show that Arthur Burch's death was no suicide.

Then from behind her, appallingly loud in the thick silence, came Major Charteris's barking voice.

"Right, then, you interfering bitch."

She whirled round to face him, aware at once that standing between him and the low moonlit window she must be outlined against the garden beyond.

In his hand she saw the glint of metal. A pistol.

But she had been ready for this or something like it, ever since she had invented for the Major's benefit a mysterious "object" he might have dropped in the cottage when he had come to kill ready-to-blab Arthur Burch.

She flung herself forward facedown towards the shelter of the clumsy old table.

And as she did so two things happened over beside the door. With a roar of sound in the low-ceilinged room Major Charteris fired his pistol. Its noise was so deafening that for a moment Miss Unwin was unable to tell whether she had been hit or not.

At the same time she had caught just a glimpse as she hurled herself down of the flash of a larger, more shining piece of metal than the Major's pistol. And, following closely on the confined thunder of the shot, there came a yelp of pain.

Then a new voice broke in.

"Stand where you are. One move and my sword runs you through."

It was the voice, Miss Unwin recognised with flooding relief, of old General Pastell. Old, but active and steely-determined still.

"Are you safe, Miss Unwin?" he asked as soon as it became clear that the man who had attempted to murder her was not going to do anything other than stay where he was, silent and baffled.

Miss Unwin considered.

She was bruised and sore, she knew. She could not have flung herself down on the stone-flagged floor so violently without suffering bruises. But, no, she was aware of no wound from the bullet that must have whistled past her.

"Yes, sir," she answered the General. "No harm done, I believe."

"You'll find matches and a candle on the table, then."

"Thank you, sir."

Miss Unwin eased herself painfully out of her hiding-place and pushed herself to her feet. She did indeed feel sore from knee to forehead, but no worse. She swept a hand over the surface of the table until it came in contact with a metal candle-holder. In it she found a box of lucifers. She fumbled with them for a little and at last produced a flare of light. She put it hastily to the wick of the candle.

By the swiftly growing flame, she saw the two men standing beside the door. General Pastell, though dressed in a suit of country tweeds and with a deerstalker hat on his head, still looked every inch the soldier. It was a picture that the heavy sabre in his right hand, its point held steadily at his captive's neck, did nothing to detract from. But Major Charteris, despite his fierce military moustaches, no longer resembled the soldier he had always portrayed himself as. Even his right arm hanging loosely by his side and softly dripping blood from the slash the General had given him onto the pistol lying at his feet did nothing to make him look like the once-wounded hero of the Battle of the Alma.

As the candlelight fully established itself, General Pastell turned for a moment towards Miss Unwin.

"Well, my dear," he said, "you look little the worse for all that."

"No, sir, I believe I am none the worse."

But then abruptly she felt the need to reach forward and steady herself by holding firmly onto the table in front of her.

The General saw the sudden movement.

"Touch of faintness, eh?" he said reassuringly. "Don't you mind it, my dear. I felt exactly the same when I dismounted after that charge they're always talking about."

Miss Unwin's spirits perked up. "The Light Brigade?" she asked. "You were in the Charge?"

"Well, yes, I was. Make too much of it all nowadays. That nonsense of a poem by that fellow. I tell you, I was damned— I beg your pardon, ma'am. I was extremely glad to find I had ridden out of it all more or less unscathed."

"And did you—forgive me, I ought to know this—did Her Majesty confer any award on you?"

"Hm. You mean the Victoria Cross, like our friend here? No, I did nothing to deserve anything like that. Can't understand why a fellow who had should take to behaving as he's done."

"I think I can give you an answer to that, sir," Miss Unwin said. "Indeed, if I am not mistaken, that Victoria Cross lies at the bottom of the whole of this business."

She then saw Major Charteris for one moment look up. And the glance that he gave her was as full of hatred as any she had ever seen.

"So you know," he spat out. "You know why I had to kill Goode, and why I had to get rid of Steadman, too."

"Yes," said Miss Unwin, "I think I have found out most of it." She turned to General Pastell. "General," she said, "you heard those words from Major Charteris. Are they enough to justify you as a magistrate telegraphing the Home Secretary?"

"They are indeed, my dear," the old man said. "And we'd best be off to see about it. I've got a groom on my best hunter waiting not far from the top of the lane, and I'll write him a message to take to Chipping Compton in two minutes."

"Then let's go, for heaven's sake," Miss Unwin said, prey suddenly to a dozen fantastic fears of obstacles rising up in their way.

But nothing, in fact, hindered their progress. The General made Major Charteris walk in front, the bare sabre at his back. Miss Unwin brought up the rear, and their strange little procession soon reached Gallows Corner, where the General gave a stentorian shout in the darkness.

Two minutes later his groom appeared, leading the fine hunter and with a lit lantern in his other hand. By it the General wrote out his message, and in a very short time the groom was galloping away with it and with instructions to rouse Inspector Whatmough, still ignorant of the whole affair, and get him to come with a party of men to effect an arrest.

Then they settled down on the grassy bank at the roadside to wait.

"Tell me," the General said, after some minutes of silence, "what was that you were saying, Miss Unwin, about Charteris's V.C. being at the bottom of it all? You mentioned nothing of the sort in the letter you sent me by Vilkins asking me to witness this business."

"No, sir, I doubted whether you would believe me. Indeed, I even doubted whether you would agree to come and witness the attempt on my life that I had to bring about if I was to get enough proof of John Steadman's innocence."

"Well, that you have, my dear, no doubt about it. And in another few minutes my telegraph message to Whitehall will be on its way. But the Victoria Cross. What do you mean about that?"

"Just this, sir. And I think now that what was little more than a guess on my part will prove after all to be the truth. All along, when I thought about that terrible trick that was played on John Steadman, I was unable to understand how it could be that he had been involved, unknowingly, in the blackmail which I was certain Alfie Goode had practised."

"I follow so far."

"Well, sir, it occurred to me eventually that all three persons in the affair might well have been soldiers together on some occasion or at some place in particular. In a manner which I prefer not to have to tell you about I was able to—shall we say?—consult files from the War Office, and—"

"That clever hussy, Mary Vilkins," the General interrupted. "She shall be rewarded, the minx, if guineas can do it."

"You know what I asked her to do, then, sir?"

"Got it out of her, didn't I, when she brought me your letter." The General chuckled.

"Well, it turned out," Miss Unwin went on, "that I was right. When I looked at that list of your military guests at the ball with the War Office clerk's notes on it, I saw straightaway that Major Charteris had been wounded at the Battle of the Alma. I knew, too, that Corporal Steadman had been in action there and, indeed, from Mrs. Steadman, that he, too, had been badly wounded and had been missing for a long period afterwards. And Goode was in the Crimea at the time. Now, I was looking for something that would have given that unpleasant person his opportunity. I didn't think any ordinary peccadillo of military life abroad would provide anything grave enough, and so it occurred to me that perhaps Major Charteris's V.C. had not been properly earned in that smoke-shrouded battle at the crossing of the River Alma."

"Oh, yes, confusion all round there. Remember it well. The Russians had set a village on fire on our left, put straw in the houses, too, I believe. You couldn't see more than five yards in front of you in places. So in that famous muddle Charteris

here never captured the Russian twelve-pounder he was
credited with, eh? Never turned it against them? Is that what
you think, Miss Unwin?"

But Miss Unwin was not allowed to answer. The wounded
man broke in, his voice harsh with bitterness.

"Yes, damn it, the woman guessed it all. No, I never captured that gun. It was Steadman, Corporal Steadman, who
did that. What I did was to run blubbering towards the enemy like a schoolchild, ready to give myself up as a prisoner if
only I could get some peace."

"A good many of us have felt the same," General Pastell
said with unexpected gentleness.

"Very well. But none of you broke as I did, did you? You
none of you went running to the enemy. To the enemy. And
were only saved from utter degradation by a corporal who
seized hold of you and dealt you a blow that left you unconscious."

"So that was it?" Miss Unwin murmured.

"Yes. And when I recovered a few minutes later, the corporal had gone and I thought I would have to surrender after
all. Until, just at that moment of all moments, the note of the
Russians sounding retreat came floating through the air as a
breeze lifted the smoke. And I—wild with relief—I leapt up
and shouted out that stupid hunting call "Stole away." And,
damn it, at that instant my colonel rode up, and afterwards
he told the story again and again, with Lieutenant Charteris
capturing that Russian gun as the start of it. And then—then
after the war Her Majesty wanted to give me the Cross."

"You could at least have refused," Miss Unwin said.

"Yes, I could have refused, and, oh, I should have, I know.
But I saw that medal as my path out of mediocrity." He
turned to General Pastell. "You purchased your commission
and your promotions, General, I suppose?" he asked.

"I did. I hope I earned them afterwards, but, like many
another, I bought each promotion step by step."

"Well, I had no family with money to do that. I knew that if nothing intervened I would hardly rise above a captaincy and would end my days a wretched half-pay officer. But the Cross changed all that, as I knew it would. Would you, as a magistrate, sir, have considered me for the post of Chief Constable of this county without those letters 'V.C.' after my name?"

"Perhaps I would not. No, I would not have done. I admit it."

"So you see why I did what I did. I believed no one, no one on this earth, knew what had really happened. I thought the corporal who had struck me down for my own honour had been killed, and I believed no one else had seen anything. And then . . . Then after twenty years that man Goode appeared here. Apparently he had been lying and skulking nearby at the battle and had seen it all. So he extorted money from me, telling me by way of precaution that he had as witness to my behavior that very corporal who had struck me. It took me months to worm the fellow's name out of Goode, but then I was ready to deal with him. He was bleeding me white, with less pity by far than I had when I made that wretched man Burch furnish that room for me. I ought to have turned him out of the farm he was so mismanaging as soon as I set eyes on him."

"And you went on to force him to give evidence against Corporal Steadman?" the General asked.

"Yes, yes. Of course. It was my plan. And then when this hussy came on the scene, he had to go. So I killed him, too. Yes, there it is. Now take me to the hangman."

Then, with no warning, the murderer of Alfie Goode and Arthur Burch pitched forward onto the grass in front of him.

Miss Unwin started back in alarm.

"No, it's all right, my dear," General Pastell said. "The fellow's only fainted. Loss of blood. Good thing, on the whole. I'm not as young as I was, and keeping my sabre point at the ready was beginning to be more than I could manage. But

Inspector Whatmough and his men should be here before long."

The General coughed then in the darkness, with something of a note of apology.

"There's something more about this that perhaps you can enlighten me over, Miss Unwin," he said. "And, please, my dear, don't hesitate to tell the whole truth."

"What is it, General?" Miss Unwin asked, though she had more than an inkling of what it was the old soldier wanted to know.

"Mrs. De Lyall," he said. "It was her that Charteris used to meet in that cottage, wasn't it? You understand, I don't want to blacken the lady's name, but the truth of all this must come out sooner or later."

"Oh, yes, I'm afraid it was she," Miss Unwin said. "But I realised that only when she came to try to chase me from the town. It was when she did so a second time and pretended then to have no liking for Major Charteris that I began thinking. She was altogether too vehement. And then it didn't take me long to see that it must be the Major whom she was trying to protect and who therefore must be the man masquerading as one Mr. Sutter at the cottage."

"I see," the General said. "But all the same, how did you go on to work out that the business in the Crimea was at the back of it all? To tell you the truth, I thought until now that female detectives existed only in the pages of sensational novels. But you've given me an altogether different impression of them. I mean, have you really studied those eight volumes of Mr. Kinglake's history of the campaign?"

Miss Unwin smiled. "No, General," she said. "I have been consulting quite another work. You see, sir, your disbelief in the existence of female detectives is, for all I know, quite justified. Certainly, I am no such person. I am no more than a simple governess, and it is to nothing more erudite than the Rev. C. P. Wilkinson's *Heroes of the Crimea*, told for boys, that I owe my knowledge of what happened in the days of the real Valley of Death."

AGATHA CHRISTIE

"One of the most imaginative and fertile plot creators of all time!"—Ellery Queen

Miss Marple

____	THE MURDER AT THE VICARAGE	0-425-09453-7/$3.50
____	THE TUESDAY CLUB MURDERS	0-425-08903-7/$3.50
____	DOUBLE SIN AND OTHER STORIES	0-425-06781-5/$3.50
____	THE MOVING FINGER	0-425-10569-5/$3.50
____	THE REGATTA MYSTERY AND OTHER STORIES	0-425-10041-3/$3.50
____	THREE BLIND MICE AND OTHER STORIES	0-425-06806-4/$3.50